Short Stories

Volu

Compiled and edited by:
Rod Griffiths, Tony Judge & Polly Robinson

With contributions from:

Mike Alma
Kevin Brooke
Tim Butler
Alan Durham
Tana Durham
Rod Griffiths
Tony Judge
Andy Kirk
Damon Lord
Alison Maynard
Andrew Owens
Dunstan Power
Polly Robinson
Suz Winspear

Short Stories from Black Pear
Volume 1

First published in December 2013 by Black Pear Press
www.blackpear.net

Compiled & edited by:
Rod Griffiths, Tony Judge & Polly Robinson

ISBN 978-0-9927755-0-6

Cover Design by Lois Parker & Rod Griffiths
Cover Image by Lois Parker & Rod Griffiths
With Worcester Black Pears supplied by
www.keepers-nursery.co.uk

Dedication

This anthology is dedicated to Lois and Radmila: up with us they put.

Acknowledgements

Thanks to all the contributors for sending us their stories and sticking with us through the vagaries of the editing process.

The Changeling by Polly Robinson was first published in 2012 in Fusion ed. Fantastic Books Publishing www.fantasticbookspublishing.com.

A shortened version of *Brick Lane Freedom* by Mike Alma will appear in the Coach House Writers Anthology 2014.

A Christmas Kiss by Damon Lord was previously published on the Spinetinglers.co.uk website as the winner of their 2008 Christmas story competition, and in the Spinetinglers 2010 anthology.

The Price by Damon Lord was previously published on the Mirror Dance website in 2009.

Foreword

Welcome to this anthology of short stories, the first publication from Black Pear Press. In 1917 Hogarth Press was founded by Virginia and Leonard Woolf to publish their own works and later those of friends. Sixty years ago T. S. Eliot founded the Poetry Book Society 'to propagate the art of poetry'. There is a fine tradition of small publishing endeavours set up by groups of friends with a common literary ethos. In this tradition, albeit without hubris, three Worcestershire writers have established Black Pear Press to offer the opportunity of publication to fellow writers.

All credit to Rod Griffiths, this venture is his brainchild. Rod asked Tony Judge and Polly Robinson to join him, and they were in business. They've been working together for almost a year, and trust you'll enjoy reading the stories, the cover artwork and the spirit underpinning their efforts.

The stories in this anthology reflect the diverse talents of people living and writing in Worcestershire, the Black Pear County.

The Black Pear Press will regularly publish novels, poetry and short stories, with some of its publications originating from the Worcestershire LitFest & Fringe.

I heartily support the Short Stories from Black Pear anthology and am honoured to have been asked to pen this foreword.

Martin Driscoll

Director • The Worcestershire LitFest & Fringe

Contents

A Bucket Full of Fish – Kevin Brooke

I was really looking forward to a bit of peace last Saturday. Dad was out of the way and Mum had gone into town with my younger sister, Harriet – she's in year eight by the way and a couple of years below me.

There was a proper storm going on outside – enough to rattle the window frames and everything – so I thought, *perfect, serious Xbox time*, when Dad comes running into my room, slamming open the door without even bothering to knock.

'Joe, you've got to see this,' he said. 'There's seaweed in the garden.'

I turned around, giving him my best *just go away* stare, but it didn't work.

'There's been a cyclone at the beach apparently and it's scooped up the seaweed,' he said. 'Guess where it's landed?'

Why was he asking me to guess? He'd told me already. God, he was an idiot sometimes.

'Aren't you coming out?'

See what I mean? Idiot. Anyway, I got out of bed; what choice did I have? You have to humour people sometimes, don't you.

Out of the kitchen door he went, wearing his dodgy looking green mac that makes him look like a flasher. He had a bucket and a small fishing net in his hands. I was about to return to my bedroom, when he came rushing back in through the door.

'Have you seen it?'

I peered out of the window, and that's when it started.

'Blimey!' There was seaweed everywhere. 'There's seaweed everywhere.'

'Told you,' he replied.

All over the fence it was, and the shed, and the lawn.

'Bloody Nora,' Dad said, jumping away from the door.

'No way,' I said.

As if the seaweed wasn't enough, it was now raining fish and other creatures. Blimey it was weird.

Dad went to the tall cupboard by the sink and pulled out a second bucket and net.

'We'd better do something,' he said. 'Come on.'

'You're joking. I'm not going out in that!'

'We'll be okay, don't you worry; it's stopping now.'

I looked out of the window again and, to be fair, apart from the thunder and lightning, the raining fish part of the storm did appear to be stopping.

The front door opened and then slammed shut.

'What the hell is going on?' said Mum, hurrying into the house.

Harriet followed her into the kitchen and I was certain she'd wander off, uninterested, and go back to her bedroom. Instead, she put on her wellies and went outside with Dad.

Amazing.

'Don't just stand there, Joe,' said Mum, as she too went out into the garden.

Incredible.

I had no choice now. Outside, Dad was on his knees, his mouth attached to the paddling pool valve. Both Harriet and Mum were running around the garden, buckets and nets in their hands, collecting fish.

'Grab another bucket from the shed, Joe,' said Harriet. 'Try not to stand on the frogs.'

There weren't any buckets left, so I tried to pick up a few of the fish with my hands, but they kept slipping out, their long tails slapping on the lawn. Blimey they stank. Eventually, Harriet took pity on me and handed me her bucket.

'What about the crabs?' I asked. 'Should I put them in as well?'

Dad shrugged. 'Why not?' he said, so I picked up a few of the crabs, trying to avoid their nippers and claws. Same with the lobsters. There were a few starfish and even a small octopus. He was a bit wobbly, but, after a few tries, I slid him into the paddling pool. The turtles seemed quite happy where they were, so I left them alone, along with the jellyfish. I didn't fancy getting stung by him.

Then things got very strange. I was going around the garden with my bucket and net, picking up the stragglers, when I noticed something big under the apple tree. Now when I say big, I mean really, really big. Huge, in fact. It was grey, about three metres long, with starey eyes, a couple of fins just behind its head and a long swishy tail. At first I thought it was a shark, but Dad soon put me right.

'Conger Eel. I've just called the RSPCA.'

I looked at the eel, flopping about all helpless, and then back at Dad. We couldn't just leave it there.

'Right, you get the tail and I'll get the head,' I said, taking on the challenge. The trouble was: the eel was just too awkward and heavy for two of us.

'Careful of those teeth,' Dad said, and I looked down just in time to avoid the eel sinking them into my arm. I was about to drop it, when Mum and Harriet came rushing over, grabbing hold of its middle.

Step by difficult step, some forward, some sideways, we headed towards the safe haven of the paddling pool, until at last we heaved it over the side with a great SPLASH!

As the eel hit the water, however, I lost my balance and fell into Mum, who toppled over, taking Harriet with her, who in turn tripped up Dad with a flailing leg.

So there we all were, collapsed on the lawn in a heap in the wet and the mud. The rain was still pouring down and it was suddenly freezing cold. We looked at each other in complete silence for a few moments until we all burst out laughing. Just then the phone rang in the house, and, as I was closest to the back door, I went to answer it.

'Probably the RSPCA,' said Dad.

It wasn't the RSPCA but my nan, who lives about a mile away from us.

'It's raining cats and dogs here,' she said, and, d'you know, for a second or two I almost believed her.

A Christmas Kiss – Damon Lord

Working the graveyard shift on Christmas Eve was perhaps the worst part of his job. So many cheery people, pumped full of excitement, and here he was, bringing tidings of comfort, but no joy. And so many sad, terribly sad misunderstandings.

He walked past the nurses' station; they were wrapping a few little presents for those small, dear ones in their care, but they did not see him. They never did. He was a regular visitor to this hospital, to this ward, but he never received even a 'hello' from the staff. It had upset him when he had first taken on the job. He expected some acknowledgement, yet now he was happy in his solitude. He could get on with his Great Work with no fear of interruption.

He stood by the battered old CD player and watched them. *Lonely this Christmas* played soft and low, just low enough not to bother patients. It kept jumping on the line 'Lonely without you'. The nurses looked up and glared at the CD player, but they were too busy to attend to it. At last one of the nurses could bear it no longer and stood up. Before she could move, he placed his long, pale, thin fingers on top of the CD player, gave it an indiscernible knock, and it went on playing as normal. The nurse went back to the presents.

'Merry Christmas,' he said, and moved on.

The girl was asleep in a side room off the main ward. It was dark as he entered. There were decorations intended to cheer her up, but the real illumination came from the banks of machines she was connected to. They flashed their green and red lights with such regularity that fairy lights were not needed. He moved into the room and sat down by her bedside. Gently, he took her hand and held it.

She had such a pallid hand; her skin paper-thin and covered in marks where nurses and doctors had jabbed needles and cannulas into her veins and arteries so frequently in her treatment. She had lost a lot of weight; she was small for her age. Her hair had been beautiful once: luscious flowing yellow locks and sweet curls framed her radiant smiling face. All that was left was a handful of lonely strands and a pink ribbon, a pitiful attempt to retain prettiness and dignity in the child. She no longer smiled, but she never cried.

She stirred.

It is almost time. She will wake soon, and it will be time.

He stood up.

She blinked, moved slightly and then opened her eyes. Her breathing was shallow. He watched her frail form struggling for each breath. She closed her eyes again.

A little while longer, perhaps?

He looked at the steady ticking clock on the wall. Second after second ticked by. It was nearly midnight.

Then she woke fully. She did not shift from her position; she did not have the energy. She looked around the room, taking in all she could in the gloom. Then she saw him.

At this stage, he would only appear as a dark shape. In the darkness of the room she would see someone but not be able to make out who it was.

'Hello?'

'Hello.' She was almost ready, so it was only polite to get things underway. 'How are you feeling?'

'I'm fine,' she lied. 'My name's Jessica.' Her voice seemed bright, but any real glow in her words was smothered by pain.

'I know. You've been a good girl this year, haven't you?'

'I've tried. Sometimes I shout when they put needles in me, but Mummy tells me to be brave.'

She closed her eyes again. It had taken a lot of effort for her to talk. He sat watching her, patient. He had time. He had nothing but time.

At last she opened her eyes again and looked at him. To her, he would still be just a silhouette, framed by the light in the hallway. A figure in black. He did not want to scare her, not at this important moment. Did she know who he was?

It was as if she had read his mind when she drew up her strength to speak again. 'Are you Father Christmas?'

'No. I'm sorry.' And he truly was sorry. 'Santa won't be visiting you tonight.'

She sighed, but did not speak. Sometimes when he told children that, they kicked up a fuss. But this girl, Jessica, had been through so much; news such as Santa not coming only more for her to endure.

'Does it hurt?' he asked. 'You can be honest with me.'

She closed her eyes and he saw hot tears well up.

'Yes.'

'I want to give you a chance to be free. You can come with me; we can go away; I can take you now and you'll not feel such terrible things again. We can see such lovely things together, and you'll feel fine again. Do you understand?'

She drew a big breath. 'Will Mummy and Daddy be going as well?'

'No. They can't come. Not for a while yet.'

She was gathering her strength, fighting the fatigue that talking to me caused. 'Can I bring my dolly?'

'No. You can't bring anything with you. Nothing. Just you. And me. And we'll go tonight.'

Seconds ticked by as she fought to speak again. Her frail form was wasted, destroyed by her illness, but still she clung on to life with all the power in her little body.

Until now.

'All right. I know you. You're the death man like in Bill and Ted.'

Bill and Ted? What was an innocent young kid doing, watching that? He wanted to laugh but did not. She had recognised him, that was the important thing, and the solemnity of her decision was paramount.

'Please take away all the bad stuff in me. Let me go with you.' She sank back into her pillows and closed her eyes for the last time. She was still, only her chest moving slightly. Her breathing became shallower, each breath becoming slower, pausing longer and longer between each aspiration.

Outside, somewhere in the distance, a clock tower on a church was starting to chime midnight. He leaned forward over her, holding her hand with his, seeking to deliver a final kiss. The bells rang on in the crisp, frozen darkness outside. He touched her gently on the forehead with his cold lips.

At once, he stiffened, a foul sense emanating from his lips throughout his body. His entire form writhed with all the woe and suffering her body had once contained.

nausea pain

ice

fire sharp

dull pounding

cutting

deep inside

hard punch thrust endless

rot decay

make it stop

make it stop

make it STOP!

The chiming of midnight suddenly ceased.

And then the pain was gone. The deed was done. He still held Jessica's hand, but she was different. She was a changed girl. She sat up and shuffled over to the edge of the bed.

'Hello, Jessica. How do you feel?'

She smiled brightly. She absentmindedly brushed her thick long golden hair with her free hand. 'I'm fine.'

'I'm happy for you. Shall we go now?'

'Yes.' She bounced off the bed, skipping around the room. 'Can I ask you something?'

They always had questions. He had considered once, when he had been collecting an agnostic, drawing up a FAQ sheet to hand out whenever he arrived. He'd thought again. It would be in definite bad taste.

'Will I see Mummy and Daddy again?'

The perennial favourite query. If it weren't a parent they would miss, it would be a spouse, or a child, a lover or a friend. Never a dog or a cat. And always the same answer. 'You can see them whenever you like. But they won't usually be able to see you.'

'Okay.' She was quiet for a moment. He led her silently over to the window. She looked back at the bed, at the now still cadaver. It had held her captive for so long in bonds of stinking torment. 'Who's that girl?'

'Oh, don't worry about her. She was unwell for a long time, but she's going to be fine now.'

She glanced at the clock high on the wall. It had stopped. 'Daddy taught me to tell the time. It's after twelve in the night-time. That means it's a new day. It's Christmas Day.' She grinned, looked at her new companion, and said: 'Merry Christmas, Death.'

'Thank you. No one's ever said that to me before.' He had other souls to collect tonight, but they could wait. 'I've had an idea. Before we go where I need to take you, let's go over to the zoo and look at the reindeer. Just remember they can't see you.'

Together they stepped right through the window-pane, and beyond. They didn't notice what was going on behind them. The clock began again and the nurses abandoned their wrapping of presents, as the machines and monitors beeped, mourned and wailed Jessica's passing.

A Done Deal – Tana Durham

The man slid the side door of his battered red van closed with a bang. He looked up and down the leafy avenue. Nobody about. A quick in and out and no one would be any the wiser.

Mrs Mather was giving her rosewood table a loving final polish as he swaggered up her garden path. He pushed the door bell and heard it chime deep within the house. While he waited he gave the property the once over.

Seen better days, but nice all the same. Should be some good stuff. He rubbed his hands and flexed his shoulders to relax himself. Old dears made him nervous. You never quite knew how they'd react. He'd had dogs set on him. One brolly-wielding old biddy had walloped his arse all the way back to his van. She'd seemed such a kind old bird too. It just went to show how wrong you can be about human nature. Still, he struck lucky more times than not.

'Where is the old bat?' he muttered, giving the bell four impatient rings. He was just sliding a pink rosebud into his button hole when the door opened an inch. A sliver of a tiny woman was revealed through the crack. He arranged his features into a warm smile.

'Mrs Mather? I'm Mr Hounsworth. I phoned about the games table?'

'Oh yes?' The door stayed where it was.

'For my daughter?' No reaction. 'You have got one for sale?' No answer. 'Your ad in the paper. I phoned earlier. A wedding present for my daughter. Your table sounds perfect.' He pulled at his collar. Could she be senile? Well he wouldn't hold that against her. 'Can I come in? Take a look?'

'You got identification? Sorry to ask.'

'Sure. No problem. Bus pass do?' The card in the plastic wallet he held up for her was authentic. It just wasn't his. It didn't matter. Nobody ever looked properly.

She opened the door wider to see it. Quickly he stepped forward into the space.

'Can't be too careful these days,' he said, flashing it past her eyes before popping it away. 'Now, how about showing me that table?'

'I suppose so. You don't look old enough to have a bus pass, or a daughter,' she said.

'Now you're flattering me. Softening me up? You're not going to take advantage of me are ya?' Taking her by the shoulders he pointed her down the hall. 'Now, what about this table? You've got my curiosity going. Bein' all coy about it. It must be something special.'

'Oooh it is. It was a wedding present to me from my late husband. We spent many a happy night playing games on it. Didn't have a telly then. It's old mind, but I've kept it nice.' She indicated the small table in the middle of the room. The rich wood parquetry glowed in the late afternoon sunshine.

Mr Hounslow walked slowly around the table, his chin in his hand. He shook his head very slowly.

'Lovely old wood,' she said, not liking his silence. 'Rosewood and something. Victorian I think. Old anyway.'

He looked uncomfortable.

'Well what do you think? Do you want to buy it? For your daughter?'

Mr Hounslow sucked breath through his lips. The head shaking increased.

'Can't, love.'

'Why not? It's beautiful.' Mrs Mather stroked the burnished wood lovingly, tracing the chequered design with one gnarled finger. 'Your daughter and her new husband could play chess or cards like we did.'

'You've kept it proper, I'll agree. It may or may not be antique. But it don't fit with the modern taste. Brown yuh see. An' cards, chess and the like …? Different games they play nowadays. Electronic.'

'But you said on the phone …'

'Now I see it though … 'fraid not.'

Mrs Mather thought, I won't plead. I'd rather keep it. On the other hand I've no one to play with now, and those bills …

'I'll see you out,' she said, making up her mind.

He made a gesture of helpless regret, took a few steps and then swung back to her.

'Now I feel bad. I didn't mean to give you false hope,' he said earnestly. 'Tell you what I'll do, 'cos you're a lovely lady and you remind me of my own gran, God rest her soul. I'll give you twenty quid for it. More'n it's worth, darlin', but I'm a sucker for a pretty face.'

'No I couldn't. I was hoping for a hundred. It must be worth that. Victorian. Good condition.'

'Well a few years ago it might've been worth more. But it's the Americans see. They don't buy since 9/11. And the recession. Nobody's buyin' here neither.'

'Aren't they?'

'Some advice for free. Try the internet. That's yer best bet.' He turned to go.

'Twenty? It's not much.'

'OK, darling. For you, thirty. Take or leave it. Deal?' He fanned out six new five-pound notes. 'Say yes and I'll take it out of your way now.'

It looked quite a lot of money. He put the notes into her hand and closed her fist around them. 'You drive a hard bargain, darlin'. I hope I won't regret this.'

She felt she needed to reassure him. Perhaps she had been too tough. 'You'll have years of pleasure, I'm sure. You'll look after it won't you?'

'With my life, darlin'. I like a game of chess mesel'. Now don't you go telling folks what a pushover I am.' He bent to kiss her hand and with a final flourish gave her the rosebud from his button hole.

'How lovely,' she said, touched by his gallantry. 'Young Love. I've one growing by the side of my front door.'

* * *

Ten minutes later Mr Hounsworth reverently placed the table before the bejewelled blonde owner of Grosvenor Antiques.

'Angela, my darling. Looking gorgeous. You're going to love me when you see this gem.' He uncovered Mrs Mather's table with a flourish. 'You got a customer what's looking for a rosewood games table ain't ya? Took a bit of tracking down and it's pristine so it ain't cheap.'

'William IV I'd say,' Angela said, failing to hide her excitement.

'Yup. Circa 1840. Rosewood and boxwood. Veneer's in perfect nick. Five hundred and it's yours.'

'I'll give you three hundred.'

'Come on, Anj. It's worth five. You'll double your money no probs.'

'Three.'

'Be fair! I gave three. I gotta make a profit. Make it four and you've got a deal.'

'Three fifty and we'll shake on it.'

'You're a hard woman, Anj. You gotta deal. Don't you be telling no one what a pushover I am.' Mr Hounsworth sighed and shook his head as Angela counted the cash into his hand.

Mr Hounsworth felt on top of the world as he eased his van into the tea-time traffic. He sounded his horn and high-fived the air with elation.

'Damn, I'm good,' he yelled out of the window.

In the shop next door to Grosvenor Antiques, an old lady was settling her newspaper bill. 'Someone's happy,' said Mrs Mather, hearing the triumphant hooting.

The assistant's expression didn't alter. 'That'll be £29.97p.'

Mrs Mather took her three pence change, looked at it and then dropped it into the lifeboat-shaped charity box.

All Inclusive - Andrew Owens

'Yeah hi, I'm calling in regards to the ad in the paper.'

'And which ad would that be for, sir?'

'The all inclusive wedding package for £3000. I was wondering if you could tell me a bit more about it.'

'Yes certainly, we provide a service for a civil ceremony in the Harriet Hall, the wedding breakfast would take place in the business lounge and the evening reception would be in the Letterworth Suite. Both the civil ceremony and the breakfast would be for fifty guests and the evening reception for seventy, but you could add to those numbers if necessary. When were you planning on holding the wedding?'

'I'm in no rush. I've waited this long. When could you do it?'

'No earlier than next year. If you are looking to hold a summer wedding, the first two weekends in July are fully booked and so is the first weekend in August.'

'Fine. So, when would I meet her?'

'Uh, who?'

'My wife.'

'Excuse me, your wife?'

'Yes, my wife. Would I get to meet her before the wedding or on the day? I'm not fussy. I've not had so much as a girlfriend before now so I don't really care what she looks like.'

'This is some kind of a joke, right?'

'This is no laughing matter. You mean to say that you don't provide partners for single customers?'

'No, we don't.'

'Well, your ad did say "everything you need for your wedding day" and I need a wife. Uh, hello? Hello?'

Antics – Polly Robinson

Babies born 'in the caul' – when their amniotic sack, or amnion, has not burst and remains intact on the baby's head or face like a circular crown – are in many instances worldwide thought to be lucky, special or protected (JSTOR: Folklore: Vol.61, No.2, p.104 in http://england.prm.ox.ac.uk/englishness-sailors-charm.html retrieved November 2011).

There I was, hurrying through Worcester Cathedral grounds, late for tea with the bishop, when something flew past my head. I ducked and looked around. A small dark figure disappeared into a grating.

The next instant another one jumped off the cathedral. A gargoyle! It launched off sprouting little arms and legs. Giggling wickedly, it scurried past to join its companion.

'Look out,' I cried, seeing another about to descend. A child laughed and pointed at me crouched with my arms over my head. The child tugged at its mother's skirt; she shook it off.

'Don't be rude, Wayne,' she said, 'the vicar's only praying.'

They couldn't see the little beasts! I pondered this, now praying fervently as another whizzed past. It tumbled by me chanting, 'Whee … born in a caul, born in a caul, you can see us no trouble at all. Wheee …' and scampered to the grating. Another followed. I looked up at the scaffolding to see if more were to follow suit. Didn't look like it. Not believing my eyes, I ran to the grating.

There the four of them sat in a circle. Tiny, childlike voices echoed up to me. 'He-he-he, we are free, we've got an hour, what can we see?' With that, they all jumped out onto the path and, holding hands, set off towards town. I had no alternative. I followed them, doubting my sanity and offering up a prayer for the bishop's understanding.

They moved fast for such little blighters. In seconds they closed on a rather large woman bending over her full shopping bag on a bench. I watched in horror as one found a stick and poked her rear with it. She jumped, then turned, her shoulders ramrod straight. Seeing me, she blushed simpering, 'Oh, Vicar!'

'Pardon me,' I said, and hurried off after the little monsters, who were well down the path, holding their sides and hooting with laughter. 'Juggernaut! Juggernaut!' they squealed, seeing one stopped at the traffic lights. Within seconds they were aboard, moving the driver's mirror. He straightened it, puzzled. They moved it again. They took his keys; the engine stopped. The lights turned green. The driver cursed, reaching for his keys. Car horns blared. Delighted pedestrians charged across the road at breakneck speed. I joined them.

The gargoyles were now by Elgar's statue depositing the keys at its base. A mother with a child in a pushchair approached. They snatched the child's lollipop. He began to scream; his mother searched the footpath for the lolly. 'What have you done with it?' she asked him crossly. The child continued to scream while just yards away the lolly was disappearing into the gargoyles' fleshy mouths.

'Yummy, yummy, yummy, food for our tummy,' they chuckled. A Labrador swerved, sensing them, his eyes popping as he pulled his unsuspecting owner into a lamppost.

A policeman strolled along heading for the snarl-up at the traffic lights. Irate motorists shook their fists at the bewildered juggernaut driver.

Another rhyme floated back to me. 'Once in every century we have a chance to dance round free. We have fun and few can see, save those who were born in a caul.'

They turned, heading for the hotel. I'd lost them. Through revolving doors I saw the four of them busily emptying a guest's suitcase. The guest had her back to them, signing in. Bras and stockings flew through the air; the gargoyles rummaged through cosmetics, smearing lipsticks, emptying bottles. It got worse when they found the talc. I dashed in without thinking and started shoving things back into the case. She turned around. Through a fog of talc I saw her open-mouthed amazement at the sight of me clutching a pair of filmy white panties to my cassocked chest. The receptionist, galvanized into action, reached for the phone. I knew just what was happening, heaven forefend!

The young woman of the underwear found her voice, 'You're a vicar! A vicar! What are you doing?'

'Don't worry, miss, the police are on their way,' said the receptionist.

The gargoyles gambolled with glee, giggling and winking. 'He-he-he, now you'll see just how long an hour can be. Back to the cathedral, that's where we'll be. ' They left.

Well ... what could I say? The police arrived. The receptionist pointed an elegant, accusing finger at me.

The policeman viewed the devastated luggage and clouded reception area, a look of wonder on his face. He shook his head, saying, 'There's something in the air today. A lorry driver threw his keys at Elgar, held traffic up for ages, now this! In public! Come along, Vicar.'

He escorted me to his car. I saw the bishop in the distance. Beyond him the gargoyles squatted by the cathedral. I looked again and they were gone as if they'd never been. Someone, as they say, crept over my grave; I shivered. 'Pon my soul, how am I going to explain this to His Grace?'

Brick Lane Freedom – Mike Alma

The dry heat of the sun bounced off the cobbles, the shop-fronts, the old industrial walls of brick, and the costers' stalls. The moving mass of brightly coloured visitors to the market was wrapped in a cocoon of well-being. The embracing hubbub reflected the mood of the place – the noise, itself, created in an artist's palette of colours – everyone and everything was warm and friendly – every jostling body was carried along on a smile and a feeling of bright, light pleasure.

As I wandered deeper into the market, the colours sharpened and multiplied, the shouts of the traders swirling and surging into the busy warmth that surrounded the scene – fun and joy ruled the day.

I wasn't really aware of the approaching, swaggering youths, clearing all before them, until a heavily tattooed arm pushed me violently sideways, catching me completely off balance and throwing me against a solid door. Like a scene from a comedy sketch, the door flew open and I was propelled inside, spinning like a top only to finish up sitting on a grubby, dusty stairway – totally disorientated as the door slammed shut. I was still full of the joy of the market and too amused by my own predicament to feel anger – it was a shame it hadn't been filmed!

I leant my elbows on my knees, rested my chin in my hands and chuckled out loud, the noise of my laughter strangely deadened by layer on layer of dust, disuse and semi-darkness. What light there was barely made it through a grimy window above the closed door and everything inside was a soul-less, muffled grey. Laughter was strangled in my throat – the noise, the fun and the joy of the market had been switched off – clinically removed in an instant. The laughter died in my throat.

A shiver ran up my spine and I leapt to my feet, turning to see what was above me on the stairs – nothing! Suddenly the shadows seemed to threaten, creeping in on my reason – another involuntary shiver ran through me.

'Must get out!' … my own words running through my head, but before I had taken a step towards the door I heard the faintest of cries, filtering through the grey, from above … or had I? A heavy silence ensued, with my own heartbeat the only presence, as I strained to hear … nothing. The shadows around me appeared to be moving and I felt a real, irrational fear – my foolish mind was taking me to places I didn't want to go and I silently cursed my stupidity. I reached out for the door handle, but there it was again – the barely audible sound of a wailing woman, and then that same, grey silence held me tightly in its grasp.

My heart was pounding and a thin film of perspiration covered my face. I wanted to get out of there, but I was frozen to the spot – someone was crying out for help and I couldn't just walk out. It was so, so tempting – the other side of that closed door was sunshine and fun – so close! I tiptoed to the bottom of the stairs, wondering why I felt the need for total silence, gripping the handrail as tightly as I could.

I crept, step by step, to where the stairs turned back on themselves, pausing briefly to listen – nothing. I looked back down into the murk, caught between going back and going on up, not even waiting for my own decision as I made my way upward, compelled by some unknown force to go on. After what seemed forever, I reached the first landing and looked down a long corridor into the gloom, closed doors either side, but so dark I couldn't even see the end of the passage. Again, I stopped – what do I do now?

A scraping noise from somewhere above made me go cold, before the silence returned to wrap me in its leaden cloak – I was afraid. I just wanted to turn and run, but I couldn't shake that awful cry from my mind and then I was being dragged upwards again, step by terrible step towards the second floor, the only sound being the occasional creak and groan of the old stairs beneath my feet, each noise amplified in my tortured head. A broken window on the next intermediate landing allowed a shaft of bright sunlight to flood the adjacent stairs, but I felt, somehow, naked and exposed in its glare as I stepped through the brightness, my shadow laying itself on the stairs above me, making me think that someone else was lurking behind me, threatening.

I reached the second floor, the cold sweat of fear pouring down my face. Halfway down the corridor, on the left, an open door shed a tired pool of light into the passageway, drawing me on. Just before I reached the open door there was a crash from somewhere above, followed immediately by a short scream. I turned and ran back down the passage – I had to get out of there.

I didn't even make it to the stairs.

Stepping down from the next flight, what light there was behind him, the silhouette of a very large man blocked my way, his stance immediately threatening.

Never mind his stance – the dull gleam of a gun barrel said so much more. My blood ran cold – what was going on? I was in the middle of a nightmare, but I was awake. I couldn't speak – I couldn't do anything but stand there, paralysed, trembling as bile rose in my throat.

Light from the broken window barely illuminated a massive, bull-neck and a fat, pink cauliflower ear, his features lost in the gloom. He turned his head slightly and his flattened, putty nose silently confirmed his boxing credentials.

The gun jerked sideways, directing me up the next flight. My silent, wide-eyed plea for release obviously didn't influence him too much, as he repeated the movement of the gun. I edged past him, eyes downcast, dwarfed by his massive bulk. He smelled of expensive aftershave and stale sweat; abject fear does funny things.

Suddenly, from above, came a muffled shot, a grunt, and something heavy hitting the floor. I stopped dead in my tracks and a gun barrel was shoved in my back, urging me on. A cry of terror rang out – a woman's voice – a desperate, heart-rending cry that was cut off as quickly as it had begun. Each step took me closer to something dreadful. Two flights up, with no more stairs to ascend, I was roughly pushed forward, along the passageway, just as a door opened and a wiry figure emerged, obviously surprised at the sight of me being propelled towards him. He slammed the door behind him, but not before I had caught sight of a terrified woman, tied to a chair, her eyes pleading but, somehow, already without hope.

The wiry figure opened the next door down and ushered me inside, where a third man was kneeling over a face-down, prostrate form, a pool of almost-black blood spreading from beneath his head, quickly soaking into the age-worn floorboards. The kneeling figure rose to face me, a quizzical look on his face. He glanced at the other two who merely shrugged – they obviously hadn't got a clue where I'd come from, or what I was doing there. I could see all three characters now, with sufficient light to identify them, in spite of years of grime and smoke on the windows.

Strange, suddenly I wasn't scared – I was completely calm. Fear is, generally, based on the unknown, and that seemed to have gone; certainty had replaced my fear.

I met his eyes – cold, black, empty pits of evil – no compassion, there – no more life behind those dead eyes than the corpse on the floor behind him. He must have been in his early forties – six-feet-plus and strong, though not bulky, with graceful hands – very expensively dressed – dark brown hair with hints of grey at the temples. The rest of his face was classically built – strong, lean, chisel-jawed, sun tanned and, with those eyes, characterless. A tiny butterfly tattoo graced his left ear lobe. As I focussed on the butterfly, he tugged at the lobe, glanced across at his wiry companion and drew his forefinger across his neck; well, that was settled then.

There was a strange, heavy silence – nothing happened. I looked at the appointed one and our eyes met – mine were steadier and less full of fear. He gulped and looked away, but only found the eyes of his boss – eyes that were used to being obeyed. He had no choice – a gun appeared from nowhere and went straight into his side pocket, like an old movie. He paused for a moment, looking round the room, as if he were seeing it for the first, and last, time.

The big lug, his expression one of injured pride, was paying no notice, whatsoever, as he fiddled with a broken nail, and the boss-man had turned his back, rifling through the dead man's pockets. Again, there was a momentary lull, until the kneeling man gave an exasperated sigh and slowly turned his head, to stare at his accomplice, his eyes carrying a dire warning – a silent threat that produced the desired effect.

The jerk of a gun-filled pocket waved me back out into the corridor, half a step in front of the wiry fellow – much taller than I had first thought. I stopped at the next door down the hallway, hearing scarcely audible sobbing from inside the room. I turned round, but my escort slowly shook his head, avoiding my gaze. Down the stairs we went – all the way down – 'til we were standing in front of the door. I felt the gun in my ribs and held my breath, waiting and wondering if I would hear and feel the shot – do you remember anything, before the final blackness descends? I didn't want it to hurt.

With the gun still in my ribs, he reached past me and opened the door. The two of us stepped out into fresh air and sunlight, and noise and colour – a moving river of brightly smiling people. I gasped the air into my lungs, shielding my eyes against the glare of the sun, amazed I was still alive, but unable to work out what was happening. Still clutching the gun in his jacket pocket, he prodded me forward, nervously glancing from side to side, looking for what?

We both saw the two policemen strolling towards us through the crowd and I felt my companion stiffen. I risked a backward glance; he looked really scared, and went white as a sheet, but he didn't falter, pressing the gun hard into my ribs, until it hurt – his message clear. He steered me away from the policemen's path, so they passed us five or six feet away, blissfully unaware. The pressure in my ribs eased and I breathed freely again. My companion dropped back a pace, but waved his loaded pocket as a warning. On we walked, till the market stalls and the crowds petered out, just before the traffic lights on Bethnal Green Road. Where were we going from here? I turned to speak to him, but he'd gone.

I was trapped in a nightmare, lost without a gun in my ribs, with nowhere to go. No matter how desperately I looked, there was no sign of him.

Free in body but not in mind, I leant heavily against a lamppost.

'Are you alright, sir?'

Cathedral Ghosts – Alison May

Prince Arthur sighed. All around him, from the nave to the cloisters, from the choir stalls to the great wooden doors, silence hung over the cathedral. The Grey Lady shuffled past, feigning not having heard his sigh. The Prince sighed again, longer and deeper this time, one of his noted begone-cruel-world sighs. Still, nobody did him the courtesy of asking what was wrong.

He hopped down from his perch atop the tomb of one of the lesser noblemen, and fell into step behind the Grey Lady. He sighed again. She turned.

'What?'

He shrugged. 'Nothing.'

The Grey Lady shook her grey head and continued on her grey walk across the floor. She would soon disappear into the sidewall, only to reappear a few moments later – apparently quite undisturbed by her jump in time and space – from the wall at the far end of the quire. And then she would continue her grey walk once again. She was the Grey Lady. It was what she did.

Prince Arthur waited for her to come around and fell into step beside her.

'Did you hear about Albyn?' she asked.

The prince shook his head. Albyn was an old ghost of the cathedral, a stonemason from the original building. Quiet chap, kept himself to himself.

The Grey Lady smiled. 'He passed over.'

Arthur gasped. Passing over was often talked about, but seldom happened. If he hadn't seen it himself, many centuries earlier, he could almost believe that the whole idea was a fairy tale. He flicked his eyes downwards and then up to the skies. 'Do we know which way?'

The Grey Lady glanced down, down, down towards the floor.

Oh dear, thought the Prince. Poor Albyn. Well, it is always the quiet ones you have to watch.

They had reached the wall again. Arthur watched his companion vanish and sighed once more. Despite the intriguing news about Albyn, Prince Arthur was not in good humour. You might, quite logically, put that down to his being dead, deceased, no longer of this plane, but you'd be wrong. Prince Arthur had been dead some five hundred years and was quite used to the fact. To be accurate, he was five hundred and eleven years in the realm of the formerly animate, or, more precisely, six thousand three hundred and thirty-seven months, or, should you prefer, twenty-six thousand five hundred and ninety-three weeks. However one looked at things, it was a frightfully long time, and by this point Prince Arthur was not merely dead; he was bored.

It hadn't been a bad afterlife, he had to concede. Certainly the battles with King John, who had, rather inconsiderately, been laid to rest in the same part of the cathedral, had somewhat marred the first two centuries, both men believing, as they did, that they held the one true divine right to the throne of England. But since the former, in every sense of the word, Bishop of Worcester had intervened in 1732; the pair had enjoyed an increasingly good-natured truce, even going so far as to enjoy a regular Friday evening poker game in more recent years. Arthur liked poker. It passed the time.

Perhaps the old King would offer some distraction from the Prince's ennui. Arthur strolled the length of the nave and knocked politely on John's tomb. Obviously, he could just saunter straight through the wall, but to do so was considered rather poor form amongst the more aristocratic spirits, and contravened the finer print of the peace agreement carved out between Arthur and King John.

The old King floated out to greet him. 'Wassup.'

Arthur winced. 'Excuse me.'

'It's street, bro. You gotta move wiv da times.'

'I'd rather you didn't.'

The King shrugged. 'You wanna keep a low profile today, bro.'

'Why?'

'Wulstan's about.'

Arthur shuddered. Wulstan was a funny old spirit, if when you say funny you mean harrowing to the very depths of one's soul. You probably don't mean that when you say funny. Prince Arthur reversed in his head, and started the thought again.

Wulstan was terrifying. A ghost of the old school in every sense: the blood curdling screams, the white vaporous visage, the chill wind that swept through the cathedral when he was around. Happily for the rest of the resident spirits, he tended to keep out of their way, vigorously haunting the cloisters during tourist season, but preferring not to engage with the other ethereal inhabitants of the cathedral. It was unusual for Wulstan to bother them.

'Why now?' asked Prince Arthur.

The old King shrugged. 'Started last night. He got all up in my face when Albyn passed over.'

'Er … up in your face?'

'Right.' The King leant on his tomb. 'Was giving it all dis attitude. Saying the passing over shoulda been him. He been here the longest. He own dis place. All dat shizzle.'

'I see.' The Prince did not entirely see. 'I thought Albyn went …' His voice tailed off and he flicked his eyes to the ground.

'True dat. Wulstan don't care which way he go. He say he just want out. He tried to get through Albyn's portal.'

Arthur nodded. He understood. One hundred and eighty-six thousand one hundred and fifty-one days quietly haunting this cathedral was starting to affect him, and Wulstan had been here a good four hundred years before that. It got to you: the monotony, the repetition, the sheer unending sameness of it all. Arthur wondered how he would have reacted if he'd seen Albyn pass over.

It wasn't the first time he'd heard stories of a spirit trying to hitch a ride through someone else's portal.

'What happened?' he asked King John.

'Wulstan not quick enough. It not right, stealing someone else's way to the other side.' The Old King paused. 'Really dreadfully poor form.'

Arthur smiled a little. 'Dreadfully poor form? That doesn't sound very street.'

'Just how I roll bro. Keeping it real.'

Arthur nodded, and set off to continue his walk around the cathedral. It was quiet today, not many livings around, and the ghosts seemed subdued. It had been a long time since the last passing over, but Arthur remembered things had been the same then. Nothing made a ghost feel more uncertain about their lot than seeing one of their contemporaries move properly to the other side.

The temperature in the cathedral dropped a little. The prince stopped and looked around. The Grey Lady was about halfway across her walk, but other than that the cathedral was at peace. Nonetheless, Prince Arthur picked up his pace. Maybe he'd go back to his tomb and have a nice rest for a while.

He started across the floor of the cathedral, passing through rows of wooden chairs laid out in anticipation of some event later in the day. He was almost at the centre aisle when he saw it. It was directly under the tower. An archway, just sitting there like it had always been part of the building. He took a step towards it. The archway, he realised, wasn't just sitting there. It was waiting. It was waiting for him. This was it. This was his moment to pass over. The years and months and weeks and days and hours and minutes of waiting were all for this. He was going to pass over. He was going, finally, to the other side.

He took another step. A blast of cold air hit him, and a scream filled his ears. He spun to look behind him. Wulstan was flying down the length of the nave towards the arch. No chance mate. This was for him. The Prince turned back towards the arch and started to run. He could feel Wulstan gaining on him, but he didn't turn back, just kept his eyes fixed on the archway and ran and ran and ran.

It wasn't enough. Wulstan's coldness passed through him a few yards ahead of the arch. There was no point running any further. He wasn't going to make it. Arthur stopped and watched. The bedraggled old spirit approached the arch. The ghoul's scream turned to a cackle, and he turned what remained of his face towards Arthur in victory. That was his mistake.

King John leapt from behind a pillar and used all his energy to throw Wulstan back from the portal. The old King stared at Arthur and pointed to the archway. 'Go on.'

Arthur didn't need telling twice. He ran straight at the portal and into its heart. The sounds of the cathedral drifted away into a faint whisper of King John admonishing Wulstan. 'Frightfully bad show, bro. Innit?'

Then everything was quiet. Arthur stopped. He was in a clean white room, lined with chairs. He looked down one wall to see Albyn sitting quietly on his own. He thought the Grey Lady had said Albyn had gone 'down'. That was a worry. He walked over to the old mason. 'Albyn.'

The old man nodded to him. 'Your highness.'

Arthur sat down. 'So where are we?'

Albyn smiled the smile of a toddler on Christmas eve. 'Oh, this is the next stage.'

'Right.' Arthur peered around the room again. There were spirits of various vintages sitting on the chairs, and at the far end of the room a desk, tended to by a woman dressed in white. He turned back to Albyn. 'And is this heaven, or …' He flicked his eyes to the floor.

Albyn laughed. 'Oh no. No. No. This is just the waiting area.'

'What?'

'The waiting area, you know, waiting for someone to come out and process us, decide where we're going and all that.'

'But I've already waited for …' Prince Arthur's voice trailed off. He'd waited so long, back in the cathedral, but there'd been friends to talk to – the Grey Lady, the Bishop, and King John. 'How long do we have to wait?'

Albyn shrugged. 'Lady over there's been here since the Great Fire.'

'The Great Fire of London? 1666?'

'No. No.' Albyn smiled and shook his head. Arthur relaxed slightly, before Albyn continued, 'Not that Great Fire. The first one. 1135.'

Arthur slumped in his seat. So this was all there was. Just more waiting. He sighed, a truly great sigh, and peered at Albyn.

'You don't play poker, by any chance, do you?'

Circus of Life – Alan Durham

The telephone rang.

The camel spat, grumbled and belched as it regurgitated another wodge of cud from rumen to mouth. A moth-eaten beast, its moulting fur hung in tatters; an incongruous ruminating giant, standing four square amidst nettles, thistles and piles of brick rubble on waste land.

A grey-muzzled zebra had, possibly in despair, turned its back towards two pot-bellied Shetland ponies. It stood head down and forlorn, its black and white striped coat giving regular shivers in the cold rain currently sweeping in waves across this desolate patch of Yorkshire's industrial past.

The ponies were tethered separately, each held firmly to a wooden post by a twenty-foot length of rope. Their sad, conditioned lives – dictated by their owner, for the giving of joy to others, in his circus ring – caused them to constantly trot the circle prescribed by their tether rope.

Upon completion of each circuit the ponies waltzed around three times and briefly bowed their heads, before trotting back the way they came to start the process over. They kept perfect time with each other.

With one exception, the only other observers of this recurring scene were two bored chimpanzees and a lone baby bear. These animals were imprisoned in separate compartments located in the front half of a shabby horse box. Each compartment had a small padlocked door and a barred plate glass window. The ramp which formed the rear door of the horsebox was down. This presumably led into the travelling accommodation for the animals currently tethered in the scrub. Peeling paintwork signs, attached to the horse box, encouraged the public to view Walensa's World Class Travelling Menageries for a fee of two shillings and sixpence.

The exceptional observer, located on the second floor of a derelict herring canning factory, was sitting on a folding canvas stool. To the rear of his observation post was an overgrown riverside wharf. Wind was gusting along the river and battering its way through the broken windows which surrounded him. His sandwich box and flask were at his feet amongst shards of broken glass and dust. A pair of high magnification ex-army binoculars hung around his neck.

He had endured his windswept and filthy roost since before dawn.

It had its advantages. The roof didn't leak in this part of the building, plus he could keep watch without others knowing.

He had a clear view of the circus field with its tatty patched khaki big top. The three flags at the top of the tent's centre pole were the only splashes of colour on its drab exterior. The Union Jack, Stars and Stripes and the white and red horizontal stripes of the Polish flag hung wet and limp.

Surrounding the big top was a fleet of lorries, generators and caravans. Most of the rolling stock featured faded signs extolling the virtues and thrills of 'Wally' Walensa's World Class Circus.

He could also see the red phone box on the edge of the opposite pavement. Further down the street was the blue gleam of his 'latest love', his 1963 Ford Consul Capri.

He had visited the phone box before dawn and lifted the receiver to check the dialling tone. He had used his pencil torch to note the number down. Ignoring the sticky handset and the almost overpowering smell of urine, he had rung his client and left his contact number.

Why had he made the call? Maybe it was to let Pete 'Drop Kick' Popski – ex-wrestler, pawn broker, money lender and all round thug – know he was on the case and earning his retainer. £100 up front and a further £200 on the successful return of Drop Kick's runaway daughter. Not much of a fee and not a job he'd wanted, but times were hard and he had to eat.

He nibbled at a corned beef sandwich, raised his binoculars and scanned the circus site. A door had opened on one of the small caravans.

'Keep focussed,' he said to himself. 'You never know, she might just walk out of that door.'

As he watched he reflected on his only meeting with Drop Kick.

'How much for you find my daughter?' had been the opener to their conversation over the counter in Drop Kick's pawn shop.

'Well it depends on where she is?' he'd replied.

'If I knew that, I wouldn't be wasting good money on the likes of you,' Drop Kick had retorted, prodding him in the chest with a dinner plate fist.

'What's her name?'

'Halina.'

'Well why did she leave?' he persisted.

'She silly cow.'

'Did she take all her things with her?'

'How should I know? You wanna look in her room?'

'Can I speak to her mother? Did she have any friends?'

'Mother dead. No friends.'

So he'd looked in her room: not much in the way of furniture; not much in the way of clothes; nothing particularly personal, just an old teddy bear with chewed ears, which he'd found tucked away under the single bed. A passport-size black and white photograph of an unsmiling girl with short hair was pinned on the wall next to a crayoned drawing.

The drawing was of a ship sailing out to sea. Strangely, a girl was swinging on a trapeze suspended from the main mast spar. The ship was flying an enormous white and red horizontal striped flag from its stern.

'What's the drawing about?'

'No idea. She always looking at it.'

'What flag is that?'

'Polish.'

'Is she acrobatic?' he'd asked, pointing at the girl on the trapeze.

'How should I know?'

'Is she sporty?'

'I taught her to wrestle but she say she hate it. Silly cow.'

'Can I have that photograph?'

'No use to me,' snarled Drop Kick, walking out of the room.

So that was that. Meeting over.

He'd taken the photograph, teddy bear and drawing, negotiated his fee, pocketed his reluctantly given advance and started asking questions around the area.

Talking with neighbours gave him several more bits of information.

The first woman he managed to chat with said, 'Drop Kick is a horrible man and a bully who's made his daughter's life a misery since his wife died. He expects her to cook his food, keep house and do God knows what else for him.'

The second neighbour added, 'He's always shouting at Halina; she's frequently in tears. He was a pig to his wife and now he's the same to his daughter. Halina is a pleasant girl but subdued and timid. Nobody in the area is surprised she's disappeared.'

The woman who ran the corner shop speculated that the poor frightened mite had run away, as the last time she had been in her shop she'd bought toothpaste, a toothbrush, a flannel and a Pak a Mac.

'Mind you,' she'd continued, 'I wouldn't be surprised if that evil pig had done her in.'

So that was all the local information he had.

He'd also been to the library and found out that the white stripe of the Polish flag was for peace and the red was for the blood spilt fighting for independence.

After further research he'd discovered that a white horizontal stripe over a red horizontal stripe was the maritime signalling flag for the letter H. *Is this relevant? Perhaps the flag flying on the drawing represents Halina's signature?*

On discovering the possible signature connection, he'd thought more about the drawing and about the girl on the trapeze. *Was he looking at Halina's dream?*

Because of these tenuous connections he was now sitting in a cold derelict building staring through binoculars at a decrepit circus which, according to its billboard posters, had an aerial act called the Flying Poles.

He'd dismissed the bumped-off theory on the premise that Popski the money lender would never part with a hundred quid for someone he knew he'd killed.

He was just ruminating on his ridiculous tendency to make snap judgements, based on gut feelings, when Halina stepped out of the caravan door.

She had a bowl of chopped apples in one hand and the hand of an athletic looking young man clasped firmly in the other. She was smiling and laughing as they ran over to feed the chimpanzees and the baby bear. They opened the door to the bear's cage and she swept it into her arms and hugged it. The bear clung to her as she fed chopped apples to it. The young man opened the chimp cage and began feeding them with fruit. Halina looked happy and completely at home.

And that was that. There was no way he was going to tell Popski he'd found her. Goodbye two hundred quid.

He wandered across the field, gave Halina her drawing and teddy bear and reassured her that he wouldn't tell her pig of a father where she was.

The telephone rang as the blue Capri drove away.

Don't Die Like I Did – Andy Kirk

There are certain things about death that you're not told, mainly because nobody ever finds out the truth until they've passed over to the other side. By then it's too late.

I found out the hard way. If I'd known then what I know now, I certainly wouldn't have topped myself.

Yes, I committed suicide. Why? Because my life had become an unbearably miserable joke; I just didn't want to live anymore. That simple.

It's bad enough going through a divorce, especially one that gets nasty, like mine did, but when *she* – my evil ex – decided to move to Scotland with her new man, I was devastated.

I didn't care about her moving away or about her new fella; it was my inability to see my kids, Jessie and Annabel, when I wanted to that really screwed me up. Just when I thought things couldn't get any worse, I was made redundant. I lost everything: my house, the company car and my self-esteem. I was left penniless and alone. I couldn't even afford to drown my sorrows. My life ground to a halt. I became an emotional wreck.

In life, I was a high-octane junkie; the more dangerous and adrenaline-filled the activity, the more I liked it. I regularly skied, snowboarded and bungee jumped. I'd even tried hang-gliding. Now, forced to sit around with nothing to do but twiddle my thumbs and brood over everything I'd lost, I decided that enough was enough.

It was time to call it a day.

I carefully considered the various methods of ending my life: an overdose, shooting, hanging, drowning, even electrocution. But with all of these methods there is a risk of failure. I had to be 100% sure that I wouldn't survive or be discovered and saved. I wanted a foolproof method of ending my existence.

Jumping off a very high cliff seemed to tick all the boxes. I couldn't possibly survive the fall (if I picked the right spot), and I knew, with my bungee jumping experience, I'd have the nerve to do it.

I initially thought of Beachy Head – a famous spot for death leapers – but, in the end, I plumped for another piece of coastline, which I knew well.

It was a secluded place, the highest point only reachable by foot. The beach – if you can call a thirty-foot stretch of boulders and shingle a beach – is only accessible for a few hours each day, reducing the chances of me being disturbed or witnessed. It seemed a perfect place to die – but I was wrong.

It took two taxis, a train, a bus, a thirty-minute walk and every penny I had to make the journey to my chosen spot. By the time I'd made it to the summit, the rain was falling in torrents.

As I stood on the cliff-edge, the cold, harsh, salty wind howled around me, pushing like huge invisible fingers egging me on, tempting me to jump. Below, the wild ocean surged in and out of caves; enormous waves the colour of slate exploded on the rock face.

I took a deep breath and allowed a slight smile to break on my lips as I scanned the horizon; the swirling blacks and greys of the sky merged with the icy-water. I smiled again – then I jumped.

I can tell you, it's true when they say your whole life flashes before your eyes just before you die – it really does. And I mean your whole life! Don't ask me to explain how my thirty-six years of existence got crammed into the few seconds it took me to plunge four-hundred feet; just believe me when I say it did. I saw my whole life in great detail from my birth right up to the very second I died. The last thing I remember was plummeting down, cold air rushing past me and an incredible feeling of exhilaration. The fall was similar to a bungee jump, but I knew this time there would be no recoil. This was a one-way ticket to the morgue.

Everything went black.

I don't know how long the blackness lasted, but when consciousness returned I found myself standing – well, hovering, actually – over the empty shell of my corpse. The blood was horrendous; it was everywhere, intricate patterns splattered across the rocks, my body smashed and contorted on the granite. My face was now a crimson monstrosity, a pulp of flesh and bone. I was, to coin a phrase, 'a bloody mess'.

At first I was horrified, lost … I couldn't comprehend what had happened. Slowly, I realised I was dead.

Now I existed as an entity in the afterlife: a ghost, a spirit, a spook, a poltergeist, an apparition – call it what you like. Whatever I was, I'd done it: I had successfully passed over to the other side.

I can't explain how you exist in this life – it's another one of those, *I don't knows* – but you do exist. You don't eat, drink or sleep; in fact you don't do much at all. You can't feel much either, and there is no sense of smell or touch. There is no physical contact with material things. Try and touch something and you merge with it, becoming part of its substance. Your body can pass through any solid object – slowly – like honey through a tea strainer.

It took some time to get used to my new state of being; a state I assumed was only temporary. I kept telling myself that this couldn't be my final resting place. I thought I was stuck in limbo, waiting to be transferred to the after-death existence that most of us assume awaits us. But I was wrong, again. This was to be my permanent new residence.

I now know the truth: there is no up or down, no heaven or hell, no light at the end of a tunnel – at least not for someone who takes their own life. It's a sort of punishment for choosing the coward's way out.

I am now trapped; an earth-bound soul, forever more.

I can move around freely enough, glide about, float upwards and downwards, but my movement is confined to a small area. I have tried to go further but I simply can't. I don't know what stops me; there is so much I don't understand about this after-life – *my* after-life.

So what about all those other souls, those who preceded me? It turns out I'm the only one who ever died in this area, with the exception of a sheep that fell over the edge recently. Now you should understand that, as well as just floating around aimlessly with nothing to do (forever), I also have no companionship at all – unless you want to consider that less-than-intelligent animal my friend.

I don't even have the ability to haunt – not yet, anyway. It's not often that anyone ventures past this spot which I begrudgingly call home. But once a man, walking his dog, appeared, and I took the chance to try a bit of haunting, just for my own entertainment. I flew through the air, doing my ghostly best to scare him, but he didn't notice me. I even passed through the man – several times, in fact. When you pass through a living body, you not only momentarily fuse with their matter but you also acquire their emotions and experiences; you feel their pain and you see their memories. But my attempts to actually *haunt* the man were to no avail. He didn't react.

His dog, however, *did* react: growling furiously, gums flaring, teeth showing, and dribbling foaming white spittle from its jaws. It was a great response, one I would be proud to have caused, but alas it was not me that sent the dog berserk: it was that bloody sheep.

I am now far lonelier in death than I ever was in life. If I'd stuck to my original plan and jumped off Beachy Head, at least I would have had plenty of company, plenty of other souls with the same dilemma.

But, I didn't. I chose a spot that I considered perfect: somewhere private to end my life and to escape the loneliness that made me feel so desperate. I thought I'd be going to a better place, a better existence. But I was wrong, yet again!

I would cry if I could, but there's no emotion, remember. If I wasn't already dead, I would almost certainly kill myself. But I am, so I can't.

I am stuck with this existence that I have, literally, *thrown* myself into. I've got a very lonely life – or should I say death? – ahead of me.

Finbar – Alan Durham

Father Ignatius held his cross high as he led the procession.

Finbar Foy followed. He liked the priest. He was worthy. He had been his link to God for the past three years. He was now part of his resolution.

Finbar knew the good father prayed for his redemption. 'But,' he reflected, 'even a priest on his knees every night doesn't always get what he hopes for.'

Finbar laughed at his thought and felt the tension rise in the three pigs positioned around him: Porky and Lardy to either side and the Grunt waddling and wheezing behind them. Finbar's eyes flicked constantly to left and right watching them. He decided to ignore them. They were not worthy. Not intellectuals. They couldn't feed his need.

Finbar licked his lips. The men on either side of him noticed. They were alert, nervous. He had that effect.

'Shame!' he thought. 'I don't care! Why should I? They never cared for me. Ah, well.'

He looked left and right again and smiled, his lips drawing back from his long white teeth. Porky and Lardy looked away, afraid to make eye contact, afraid his cold blood-specked eyes would see their fear, afraid his smile would taint their lives.

He remembered the meal he'd just eaten. *It had been good to eat proper food again. He'd gorged on the raw liver and kidneys.*

When he had finished his meat he'd licked his plate, his tongue shooting rapidly out and in as he lapped up the congealing blood, his eyes watching the others as he drank. He'd enjoyed the taste of the offal, almost as much as he'd been delighted at the revulsion of his observers.

'Ah! The simple pleasures of life.'

He looked beyond Father Ignatius to the window at the end of the long corridor they were processing along. The sun was rising above the chipped wooden windowsill.

'Sun shining on the righteous, Father?' he questioned the priest.

'The Good Lord shines his light on us all, Finbar.'

'Even me?'

'Especially you.'

'Thank you, Father,' he replied politely. He needed everyone to relax if he was to fulfil his resolution.

'Can I have a blessing before I go?'

'You can.'

'Thank you, Father.'

They entered the execution room. The electric chair, the only furniture, stood on an insulated plinth. A large switching mechanism was fixed to a wall.

'Into the chair, you murdering bastard,' snarled the Grunt, his gummy mouth, as always, working on a plug of tobacco.

Finbar smiled at the Grunt and sat down in the chair. The guard looked away and hawked onto the floor.

'Cuff him,' said the Grunt, spraying spittle across the room and wiping a trickle of tobacco dottle from his chin with the back of his hand.

Finbar positioned his legs and arms next to the cuffing mechanisms, and Porky and Lardy fastened them securely.

'Thank you, boys,' he said, 'I hardly felt a thing.'

'Cap him,' ordered the Grunt, indicating the metal head cap fitting fixed to the chair back.

'Could I have my last blessing before you cap me?' Finbar asked, looking towards Father Ignatius.

'You may,' said the priest, holding his hand up to stop the capping.

'Thank you, Father.'

As the Priest moved towards him, Finbar bowed his head and sat quietly awaiting his blessing and the fulfilment of his resolution.

'I'm going to give you a salvation blessing. Is that OK?'

'Perfect for the occasion, thank you, Father.' He looked upwards, smiling at his priest.

'Heavenly Father, in the name of Jesus Christ,' intoned Father Ignatius, his right hand moving forward to touch the top of Finbar's head.

The priest's words 'I present this sinner to you' were cut short as Finbar swung his mouth rapidly upwards. He grasped his priest's little finger with his teeth and bit hard through the skin and into the bone. He tasted the precious blood as it flowed into his mouth.

Finbar was elated. He didn't hear the terrified screams from Father Ignatius. He didn't notice the guards desperately trying to separate him from his priest. He kept biting. He didn't hear his priest's sobbing and anguished cry of loss for his finger. He didn't hear the Grunt shouting, 'Cap the bastard now.' He didn't see his priest desperately binding a handkerchief around the stump of his finger.

He'd done it! His final resolution to die with the blood of a priest on his lips was achieved.

A successful culmination to his life's work.

His intellectual and spiritual needs were finally met.

He chewed on the finger and licked his lips to taste the blood again. His joy overflowed into euphoric laughter, and as he opened his mouth blood flowed down his chin. The mangled remains of the finger dropped into his lap. His cackling laughter echoed around the room, chilling his audience with horror and revulsion.

His demented cries of joy turned into hideous screams and only faded as the electrically induced convulsions shook and racked his body to its final rest.

Apart from the heaving sobs of the shocked Father Ignatius and the wheezing of the Grunt, the room was silent.

Finbar the Cannibal was dead.

In Vino Veritas – Damon Lord

Dawn still lurks an hour away, but this early winter morning I don't fear the approaching sun. I have plenty of time, yet I want to get this over with as soon as possible. I shuffle forward, keeping pace with the queue.

It is foolish to have come here, to risk my life, or un-life, as I prefer to call it. I should retire to my coffin early, but I must do this one last deed. I need to see if things really *can* change.

The building is magnificent, the architecture painstaking. You can feel the justified pride radiating from every stone, and the professional honour of the long-dead masons who crafted this temple to God.

I glance into the shadows at the confessional. I haven't entered a church in many, many years, and even longer has passed since my last confession. I can't stop a wry smirk from creeping across my face as I imagine my sins pouring out, should I step inside: 'Bless me Father, for I have sinned. I have murdered thousands of people in my way across the planet for the last eighty-six years since my death, and enjoyed drinking the blood of every last victim, suckling on their necks to satiate my thirst, for I am a vampire.' I'd cackle like Bela Lugosi to complete the illusion.

What am I trying to prove by being here? Who am I trying to prove it to? The others in my Nocturnal Family are already resting; they don't have the bravery, or stupidity, to step inside a holy place like this. They fear crosses and other religious icons, but I see them for what they are, mere symbols. Even amongst vampires it's a little known fact that a crucifix, or any other token, wielded without faith has no effect on my kind. Only belief gives the symbols power. The others, still freshly born into darkness, don't know this, and they fear. As for me, I like crucifixes. I have seen some beautiful ones on my travels, but I no longer fear any of them, even those imbued with credence.

There are now only a few people between me and the priest. I don't know what I'll do when I face him. Will I look him in the eye? Perhaps I'll combust. Or perhaps I'll take the priest, wring his neck, and drink from him.

I must know.

One person remains before me. In my youth, before I embraced the Night, I had faith in a God, and regularly attended and believed in the transubstantiation at Mass. Now I am a creature of the dark, destined for damnation in exchange for my choices. Yet something from those days still piques my curiosity. I now risk it all to see what it is like to partake in the Eucharist once more.

The crucifix towers above the altar, and I examine the face of the man on the cross. It is a delicious piece of art. All the pain and suffering that Jesus had taken on is displayed there in front of me; the fear and terror in the eyes of my many victims pales in comparison with this depiction of the savage reality of a holy event two millennia ago. In the stern, knowing face, the artist has somehow conveyed a piercing message of love, understanding and forgiveness.

I stare long at Jesus; Jesus gazes back. For a moment I stand far away, on a dusty hill in the midst of darkness on a hot Friday afternoon. The wind whips me, as voices chatter away around me in Aramaic, Latin, Koiné Greek, Hebrew and other tongues.

The priest coughs. His voice returns me to the now.

'The body of Christ.'

And now I grasp the Host in my hand. Is this the end? An object so holy touches me. I am a fragment of obscurity compared to this.

I do not erupt into flames.

'Amen,' I whisper. I pretend to eat the wafer, and then slip it into my pocket. As a vampire, I am unable to ingest solids. I've tried it. It has side effects, and, trust me, you never ever want to see a vampire vomit.

I glide towards the old lady who is holding the wine. The pulse throbbing in her neck sets a lust in me I struggle to contain. I restrain myself from dining on her. Instead I snatch the goblet she holds out to me.

'The blood of Christ,' she says.

'Amen,' I mutter. The first sip, tasting of sweet grapes, makes me squirm for a moment; my body prefers the salty, metallic tang of blood and the life-warm feeling it gives. I suppress an urge to gag. I lurch away, and lean into the wall, beneath one of the Stations of the Cross. I gulp, and the taste is gone.

I stumble to the rear as the wine slinks to the foul pit of my stomach. The griping reaction against its sweetness disappears and a glow of life bursts within me, spreading its warmth like the sweet, gentle nourishment of blood. I dare dwell no longer, should the transubstantiation of wine into blood be repulsed by my damned soul and revert to wine. I fear my blood-depraved carcass will foul the sacred drink.

'The blood *is* the life,' I pray, as I flee the church.

Lessons – Rod Griffiths

When I was six, I found myself in the class of a teacher who I shall call Mr. Mean to avoid any risk of legal repercussions. I did once seriously consider trying to find his grave in order to dance on it, but I've never discovered any science to suggest that this achieves anything.

Among his many foibles was an absolute dedication to calligraphy. He insisted that all children in his class must learn the style endorsed by Alfred Fairbanks. For those not familiar with it, it is an italic style, in which the letters have a pronounced thick and thin stroke.

All the children were required to write with special, square-leaded pencils. They had to be sharpened in a special way with a special knife on a special stone kept at the front of the class. The pencil had to be held at a precise angle, both when sharpening and when writing, to produce the correct shape characters.

I guess I was supposed to learn to write beautiful script, but what I acquired was a respect for sharp instruments and the knack of steadying my hands to make a precision cut; both skills that proved very useful many years later in the short period when I was an assistant brain surgeon, and almost as soon as I arrived at medical school, my terrible handwriting rapidly convinced any doubters that I was born to be a doctor.

Reading and writing were difficult for me back then. I've since discovered that dyslexia runs in my family, but none of that was known to Mr. Mean. The Fairbanks writing style gave Mr. Mean super powers: not only must the right letters be in the right order, but they also had to be the right shape. Mr. Mean had three chances to tell you that you were wrong. I was always wrong.

He had turned writing from a method of communication into something approaching a religious ritual in which heretics like me were cast into outer darkness, or more accurately, not allowed to do joined-up writing.

I suppose this could have been a considerable handicap because my immature handwriting made it seem that I was under-performing for my age. In fact, what I learned was that it did not matter what you wrote. What mattered was how you wrote it; in other words:

'It ain't what you say, it's the way that you say it.'

The appropriate response should have been to write a song, but that particular hit had already been written a dozen years earlier.

Each term all the classes across the school had to do a standard test; I usually came in the top three of the class. When the marks were announced, we were put in groups; the top eight children were in group one and my marks should have put me there.

When my turn to be selected arrived, Mr. Mean would announce to the class:

'Oh we can't have you in group one can we. Go to group two.'

A similar ritual accompanied selection of Group Leaders, a role normally allocated to the student with the highest mark in the group. When I was identified as the student with the highest marks in group two, he would announce, again to the whole class:

'Oh we can't have you as Group Leader can we.'

I never understood why I was victimised in this way; I doubt if any six-year-old could.

I found myself completely incapable of explaining any of this to my parents, and so I learned to lie. If asked about school, I said everything was fine. I achieved almost complete separation in my mind between the world of school, where nothing made sense, and the world at home, where I was loved and encouraged. Nothing from school went home; nothing from home went to school.

This caught up with me when we came to the school trip. Each of us had to bring two shillings to pay for it, but I never remembered to ask my mother for the money. Every school day we would be asked for the money and every day I realised that I had forgotten. I never did remember; the simple task of bringing two shillings from my world at home to the alien one I lived in at school was more than I could manage. Mr. Mean threatened that the whole class would not go on the trip if I did not bring the money, but still I forgot.

Looking back now, I wish I could say that I was making a protest, but I know that I did not then have the wits to achieve anything so focused.

Who knows where it might have ended if all those children who had paid, whose parents were expecting them to go on a trip, found that the trip was cancelled because of me. Would Mr. Mean have talked to my parents? Would some external power have questioned his methods? I never found the answer because on the last day another girl brought the money and forced it on me. I remember it clearly; she did it while we were sharpening pencils. I wish now that I could remember her name.

I should have learned to be ashamed that I was so incompetent, but the lesson really is this … Hold out long enough and someone else will crack.

Eventually, I passed an exam for another school. When this became known, Mr. Mean announced to the whole class:

'I will be glad when you've gone.'

And one of his teacher's pets said, 'So will I.'

'And so say all of us,' said Mr. Mean.

It is hardly surprising that I can remember this entire trauma in detail, sixty years later. I could tell you exactly where I sat as each insult was delivered. I still find it astonishing that a teacher could misuse his power and bully a six-year-old. I doubt if I will ever make sense of any of it, but the important thing is to reflect on what I learned.

I discovered an ability to put difficult issues out of my life and construct alternative realities in which the pain goes away. It is a useful talent, though I have heard of children who developed multiple personalities when confronted with similar impossible situations. Fortunately, that never happened to me.

'Says, you.'

'No it didn't.'

'Yes it did.'

(That part works better in the performance version.)

I have no idea what he hoped to achieve by his bullying, but I learned four important lessons:

– Sharp tools are useful if handled with precision and care.
– It ain't what you say, it's the way that you say it.
– Hang on long enough and someone else will crack.
– When all else fails – construct alternative realities.

Lucky Scalp – Alan Durham

Lucky pulled the wagon into the shade at the side of the ravine. He climbed stiffly down, grabbed a hessian sack and rubbed old Joe's flanks. He strolled to the tailgate, untied a bucket and slopped a little water from the butt into it. As he bent to place the pail in front of old Joe, his eyes scanned the scrubby hillside at the end of the ravine.

'Yup', he said to old Joe, 'he's with us again.'

The Indian was standing amongst the scrub, his pony nearby. They both looked as arid and dust covered as the land.

Before he'd been scalped Lucky was just a cow hand, a trail bum, drifting along in the muck and flies behind slow moving herds of Long Horns. A man of no consequence.

When people saw him now, they remembered. They could never forget the wide ragged hair-free scar and the puckered, dragged skin which ran from the crown of his head, behind his right ear to his neckline. They told him he was lucky to survive a scalping.

Along with his hair he'd lost his previous identity, but he'd gained another: everyone now called him Lucky Scalp.

The Indian had been around for about a week, seemingly drifting along with Lucky as he did his calls for Rob Harcourt the general merchant in Dry Creek. The occasional haulage work helped Lucky to scrape a living.

The ravine was cool and harboured some low-lying scrub for old Joe to nibble. Lucky decided to camp for the night. He unhitched his horse and tethered him with a long rope to one of the wagon's wheels. The Indian didn't look like a threat.

'Anyway', Lucky thought, 'what have I got worth a damn?'

He looked at his old wagon with its sagging bottom and patched sides. His Winchester had a split stock held together with tightly wound string. Old Joe was ancient and broken backed with worn down teeth.

He was sure the rolls of barbed wire he was hauling for Harcourt to Jim and Emma Jenkins were of no use to the Indian.

'Maybe he's just hungry', thought Lucky, as he pulled a jack rabbit he'd shot earlier from under the driver's bench.

He gathered some dead scrub and lit a small fire. He skinned and gutted the jack rabbit and skewered it with an iron spit he carried in the back of the wagon.

When the rabbit was cooked he chopped off the rear quarter, walked along the ravine a little way towards the Indian and hung the meat on a piece of thorn scrub.

The Indian didn't move.

The next morning the meat was gone. A handful of berries lay on a flat stone nearby.

Lucky gathered the berries and hitched up.

He had been on the trail for a couple of hours when the bullet hit him.

The impact threw him back in his seat and then the shock and pain made him slump forward. Old Joe stopped when the reins went slack.

'Get off that heap of junk you call a wagon, you bastard,' someone snarled. 'It's time me and the boys had ourselves a wagon roast and got rid of that range-choking wire you're taking to those settlers.'

Lucky clutched his shoulder and looked up at the riders surrounding his wagon. Bandanas covered their faces and Stetsons were pulled low over their eyes.

Lucky dropped his arm towards his Winchester. A lasso fell over him. He was hauled from his seat, landing heavily on his wounded shoulder. The rope tightened, dragging him through the dirt toward the rear of his wagon.

'Pete, take him for a ride up and down the trail; let's take some more skin off him,' yelled the same voice.

'My pleasure, boss,' said the rope handler.

The arrow hit Pete in the throat and he fell to the ground making choking noises, blood pouring from his mouth. The rope holding Lucky went slack.

'Christ! Indians,' yelled the boss. His warning cry turned into a scream of pain and rage as an arrow hit him in the thigh. He turned his horse and galloped away in a cloud of dust, with the other riders following him.

The dust settled and Lucky sat up looking around. The trail was empty apart from his wagon, a loose horse and Pete lying in a pool of blood. The Indian was surely watching from among the scrub which lined the side of the trail, but Lucky couldn't see him.

'Thank you,' he shouted, as he struggled to his feet, casting off the lasso. 'I don't know why you did it. Thank you anyway.'

Lucky checked old Joe and was relieved to see he was unscathed. He tied the loose horse to the tailboard, soaked his spare shirt in the water butt and wrapped it around his shoulder.

Pete was clearly dead, so he covered him with stones as well as he could with only one arm. He hoped this would keep the coyotes off until somebody collected or buried the body.

Lucky crawled back onto his wagon and told old Joe to walk on.

Another few miles and he pulled off the trail and headed towards the Jenkins place. Lucky was slumped in his seat from loss of blood. He was holding the reins but old Joe was plodding along doing all the work.

Emma Jenkins saw Lucky was injured and hurried out to help him down from the wagon.

'Jim,' she yelled at the top of her voice,' Lucky's here and he's been shot.'

'I've seen worse,' she said, as she bathed and dressed his shoulder wound. 'Bullet's gone straight through the muscle, missed the bone.'

'It seems you've brought company,' said Jim, nodding through the window towards the Indian sitting on his horse near the homestead gateway.

'Shall I run him off?'

'No leave him alone! Without him I'd be dead on the trail and your wire and my wagon would have been burnt. He seems to be watching over me but lord knows why. The last time I had anything to do with an Indian was the devil who started to scalp me, before I was dead. I took him by surprise when I stuck my Bowie knife between his ribs. Killed him and left him still clutching my scalp in his hand.'

Emma smiled at Lucky's understatement of a nasty trail fight from which he had taken months to recover.

'Could you spare some food for him? You can see his ribs.'

'Sure', said Emma, 'I'll ask One Feather our yard hand to take him some. He's half Indian and should be able to talk the language.'

One Feather walked slowly across the yard to where the Indian was sitting. After some conversation the Indian took the food, turned his pony and faded away into the scrubby landscape.

One Feather came into the farmhouse. 'He's Comanche[1]. He's called Snake Eyes. His father, Two Bears, was the brave who scalped you and you killed. To die in battle with the fresh scalp of an enemy is a great honour. Two Bears now lives forever in the happy hunting grounds in the sky.

'The Comanche also honour you for killing their great warrior Two Bears, when you had blood in your eyes from losing your hair.

---

[1] *The Comanche (ke-manchi)...a North American Indian people who ranged the western plains from Wyoming to Texas. They now live in Oklahoma.*

Snake Eyes is proud to have you as his brother, and he thanks you for sharing your meat with him.'

Montmartre Redemption – Tony Judge

He parted the heavy, velvet curtains, briefly scanning the street outside. This habit from the old days was not so necessary now, but part of a routine he was loath to discard. His habits gave him structure; structure he needed to fill his days. The new identity suited him perfectly. It shielded him from the minor spooks and press hacks, with their intrusive, impertinent questions. They had dogged him during his earlier incarnation in Brussels, gradually making his life impossible. Now he was just an old military man living in genteel retirement in a comfortable district of Paris. He rented an apartment on the lower slopes below Montmartre; nothing too showy, or that would attract suspicion. If anything, it was a little down market for his tastes, but, as his minder from the security service had pointed out, we all have to make compromises in life.

Whenever he went out, he made sure that the communal stairway was empty of any neighbours. He might see the cleaner, a pretty young African woman, who greeted him with a nod, but kept her eyes lowered as he passed. Descending the stone stairs from his apartment each day, he would perform his ritual walk, up through the old cobbled lanes to the summit of Montmartre. There he would mingle with the crowds of tourists, jostling each other outside the cloned pavement cafes – with identical menus and décor – and in the many tat-art shops. It amused him to watch the same stream of humanity rippling and eddying against the stone buildings; only their faces changed. He felt at ease there, secure in his anonymity. One dark-skinned face was unremarkable in this Babel of global tourism. Killing time, sitting on his favourite terrace and savouring the great open vista over the city, he felt nostalgic for the expansive landscapes of his homeland.

On Sundays he would make a special detour to a small stone church tucked away among the back streets, just off the main tourist trails. His Catholicism was another habit he had never quite relinquished. It had waned during most of his adult life, but now, as he approached his dotage, it came back to him, stronger and more insistent than before. As a young boy from an impoverished family, the priests and nuns of the missionary school had bestowed on him the incomparable gift of a sound primary education. Without it he would still be herding cows, sitting on the stump with his cronies, telling tall stories and sucking on his few remaining teeth. But he had been steered away from this easier, more homely life and marked out for distinction. There had followed a secondary education, then a scholarship to and graduation from a French military academy. He had returned home to prosecute a stellar army career, finishing his time as a General, with the grand title of Commander of the Eastern Regional Peoples' Militia.

He always sat at the back of the church. When the other members of the congregation rose and filed to the front to take Communion, he would remain seated. What was it Father Sébastien had drummed into them? 'You must not take the host if your conscience is burdened with a mortal sin. First, you must repent, confess your sin, accept your penance and only then are you fit to receive the sacrament.'

Confess? There was no confessional, no priest robust enough to withstand what he could confess. Besides, that would mean delving into buried memories. He had stashed them away so deeply – almost beyond recall – as deep as his treasure trove, the life-saving diamonds that had made possible his escape and now sustained him from their safe haven in a Swiss bank vault. The darkness at the rear of the church was his natural domain and, given the impossibility of confession, the sacrament would always be denied him.

He had lived this new shadow life for some years now. Even his much-shunned neighbours had started to recognise and greet him: a nod from them and a doff of the Homburg from him, but nothing more intimate than that. Intimacy was another buried memory. When was the last time? A long time ago, and even then it could hardly be called genuine intimacy. He remembered watching the woman's behind as he followed her up the stairs to her tiny apartment and tried to guess what her fee would be. Haggling, or even enquiring about the price beforehand, was beneath his dignity. Lately, his desire even for this form of release had dissipated.

Another Sunday, and he was attending mass in his usual church. The service finished and the congregation began shuffling out of their pews towards the exit. He waited until the church was nearly empty before he moved, thereby avoiding the risk of an unwelcome encounter. As he rose from his seat, he noticed, standing in the aisle near him, a young African woman. She wore a multicoloured headdress and a long overcoat. He would have left her unheeded, but sensed that she was staring at him. Turning to face her, he recognised the cleaner from his apartment block.

Slowly, she reached up and unwound the headdress until her head was bare. Even in the half-light of the church her wounds were visible. A broad, pink scar ran across her scalp from front to back and part of her left ear was missing. He recognised these as the indelible stigmata of a machete.

This time she did not avoid his gaze. Her eyes, normally so expressionless, glinted as keenly as the blade that appeared from under her overcoat. The thrust was practised perfection; the steel entered under his ribs and ignited a fire deep inside his chest. He collapsed back onto the bench, noting with detached, professional admiration: a fatal wound with a single blow. How many of his young militia girls could have performed that manoeuvre so well?

She fled down the aisle to the side exit crying unrestrainedly and shouting back at him. 'For Marie! For Papa! For Maman, Father Sébastien and all the others!' The church door slammed and he was alone.

As the blood ran between his fingers, he recalled the last image he had of Father Sébastien. The priest was spread-eagled, dead and bloodied, on the altar of his little church, as though still ministering to his flock. Their corpses were piled three and four deep on the benches in front of him. This was how the poor young scholar had repaid his teachers: with a visit from one of his elite units.

His hand fell limp at his side and his breathing became inaudible and then ceased. The red sacramental wine dripped off the bench and collected in a pool on the stone floor of the little church.

No Regrets – Andrew Owens

Where am I? What time is it? I leant up. Suddenly, I became aware of the pounding in my head. Not just yet then.

I looked to my right. No clock. Of course not, it's not my house. Who's house is this? How did I get here? The ache in my head convinced me to stay put.

I scrambled my hand along the bedside table and found my watch. 4:20am, shit.

I slipped my watch on. I heard a groan to my left. I looked over and discovered a naked woman beside me. I smiled. Got to do something about this head.

I got out of bed as quietly as I could and snuck out of the room. The bathroom was directly opposite. I closed the door and turned on the lights. Man, that's bright. I opened the medicine cabinet and to my relief there was plenty of paracetamol. After taking two tablets, I drank from the tap. Never had water tasted so good.

I turned the tap off and looked in the mirror. My bloodshot eyes gazed back at me. The water helped, but a few more hours of sleep wouldn't go amiss. Do I slip back in bed? No, I need to get home. At least there I won't get disturbed. Who was that girl? I didn't recognise her. Should I leave a note? No, I'll get dressed and see myself out. It's probably for the best.

I turned off the light, snuck back in the bedroom and quietly picked my clothes off the floor. After pulling my jeans on, I walked to the bedside table to retrieve my wallet. I looked inside. Not a single note.

I looked at the girl on the bed and smiled again. Since breaking up with my ex, Julie, sex had been hard to come by. Unfortunately, I couldn't remember it. Still, I'm sure I must have enjoyed it.

She rolled over and I admired her breasts. What a set. She brushed her hair from her face. Fuck! It is my ex! What have I done?

Suddenly, the recollection of the whole night came flooding back; the quick drink after work, bumping into an old friend, following him to a club, and the party. It was there that I ran into Julie. She was drunk and began to crack on to me. Then I remembered something I said.

'Julie, if the continuation of the human race depended on the two of us, I'd let mankind go extinct.'

Why didn't I just leave when I saw her? Why did I have to keep drinking? Whatever possessed me to get back into bed with this woman I despise? I sure hope I wore protection. I can't see anything about. What if she's given me a disease, or worse, she comes to me telling me she's pregnant? You fucking idiot, how do you keep getting into this kind of mess? I got to go.

I marched out of the bedroom and down the hall. The corridor opened into an immense lounge. There were bodies and empty cans strewn about the floor. I made my way to the front door through a minefield of debris.

Leaning against the door was the largest man I had ever seen. He had sick all down his shirt and someone had put make-up on his face. I tried to shift him, but quickly realised it was no use. Everyone else was in a similar state. There was no other way out of the apartment. I'd have to wait until morning.

Maybe I deserve this. Maybe if I wasn't such an idiot my whole life, then I wouldn't find myself in this predicament. Maybe if I had paid Julie more attention, we wouldn't have split up. This is my fault. I'm useless.

No, I'm talking shit. I need sleep. Maybe I'll just crash in here. I don't want to crash in here. Fuck, back into bed with Julie.

When I got back to the bedroom, Julie was still asleep. I opened the wardrobe. It creaked loudly. I winced and pulled out a spare duvet and spread it out on the floor.

'You don't have to do that, Jim. You can come back to bed if you like?' Julie said unmoving.

'No, it's fine. I can't. It's one thing to sleep with you when I'm out of my head, it's another to do so sober,' I replied digging out a spare pillow.

'We didn't do anything,' she said as she sat up. 'You were already passed out, when I climbed in with you. And I certainly wasn't going to sleep with you after what you said to me.'

'Then, why …?'

'I was too drunk to get home on my own and I didn't feel safe out there. Some huge guy was trying it on with me, before he got sick on me and himself. I had nowhere else to go. I know you hate me, but surely you don't hate me that much.'

'I don't hate you,' I replied, sitting down on the corner of the bed. 'It takes two to tango and maybe I'm as much to blame.'

'It wasn't you who cheated.'

'No, you've got that right. Have you any idea how much that hurt?'

'Yes I do.'

'Like fuck.'

'Yes I do. I still love you and I know I can never get you back. I wish I could erase what happened, but I can't. I've got to live with it and it's sure to haunt me for a very long time,' Julie said, and started to cry.

'I shouldn't have said what I said. I'm sorry,' I said, climbing back into bed. I pulled her towards me and cuddled her. 'You're right, we're never going to get back together, but we don't have to go on as enemies. I do still care about you and I'd like to think that one day you'll find someone and be happy.'

'Thanks, Jim,' she replied, as I kissed her on the head.

'If it makes you feel any better, I wouldn't let the world go extinct.'

I smiled and she giggled.

'Goodnight, Julie.'

'Goodnight, Jim.'

Picking a Quarrel – Mike Alma

Choosing to live in an old, dark house with a deaf, almost totally blind son may seem thoughtless, but Ben loved the place and moved around as though he had perfect vision. The windows were small and the diamond-shaped leaded lights didn't allow daylight to enter without a struggle.

Ben's favourite occupation was perching himself on the window seat in the front room, forehead resting against the lead came, with his 'better' right eye a fraction away from the rippled, irregular glass – always the same window and always the same diamond pane. A tiny parallel imprint of the lead, where he rested his head, became a permanent blemish on his right temple – a testament to the hours he spent separated from the outside world by the width of an old, imperfect piece of glass.

Only he knew what he saw through that single pane – not much according to the doctors – but whatever it was, it gave him a wonderful, almost palpable serenity that he shared in his silent, smiling presence.

Ben was only twenty-eight when he left us. We had known for years what was likely to happen; his heart just stopped beating one day while he was sitting on his window seat, head resting against the came, his beautiful long lashes brushing the glass. There was nothing we could do – I didn't even cry right then, but carried him to his room, laying him on the bed with gentle care. I kissed his temple, feeling those parallel blemishes against my lips; his face was at peace … he had suffered no pain.

His funeral wasn't for mourning but was a celebration of his life – our attempt to repay some of the many, many smiles he had gifted us during his remarkable existence – a very special human being.

Now, when I miss him too much, I sit on his window seat and gaze through that amazing pane of glass, called a *quarrel*, though what I see remains our secret – his and mine.

Rumplestiltskin 2014 – Dunstan Power

Thursday

'Ehhh, sexy lady, op … op op—'

Sarah Knowles rummaged through her bag for the mobile.

'Hello?'

'Hi Sarah? Derek.' Sarah's heart sank. What was it this time? 'Darling, listen, I have a fabulous assignment for you. This could be just what you've been looking for. How would you like to be a high powered PA? A chance of travel.'

Derek's assignments. What had they been? A receptionist at a fish-canning plant in Aberdeen; the 'Fabric Qualifier' removing exotic dead bugs from imported pants; then there was the parking attendant job at Luton airport … 'Go-on Derek. Sounds interesting,' Sarah said, feigning enthusiasm.

'It's maternity cover for the PA of the head of Luton Town Council's planning department. Thought it would be right up your street, excuse the pun.' He chuckled. 'What with your town planning masters and those hot IT skills, you're perfect. What do you think? Thing is, darling, I must get back to them straight away. They've been let down by their usual agency and need someone to start tomorrow at some conference.'

'Tomorrow? But, I—'

'I understand, previous commitment, it's OK, I'll try—'

'No, no, I'll take it.'

'Great, that's great! Get into those public-sector places, and jobs abound; it could lead to wonderful things! Good for me too, get in with a big employer and all that. I'll call back later with the details. Pack your bag.'

Sarah stared at her phone's screen. Unbelievable. Derek offering something good and in tune with her CV. She switched to her Facebook app: 'Just been offered a job – accepted. Luton TC though ☹ Anyone know anyone there?' A quick tweet too. Someone was sure to know about the place.

She needed this job; there was only so much lounging around a twenty-three-year-old could do and those travelling debts had to be paid off. She hoped her CV embroidery wasn't about to backfire though; surely a PA wouldn't need to know anything about planning?

An hour later Sarah was back at her shared flat throwing things into a suitcase. Kirsty's voice drifted from the lounge, 'When are you back? You'll be at Tanya's on Saturday?'

'No idea.' She couldn't believe how many things with sockets she had. They formed a tangle in front of her like a squashed tarantula. 'Camp Derek didn't say.'

Kirsty appeared in the doorway, mug of tea in hand. 'Well, let me know if you want your room let out; don't want any more IOUs really.'

'C'mon—' Sarah's phone sang 'Gang-Nam Style'. 'Hi, Derek, yes, OK, Birmingham? Where? Just a minute.' She grabbed a pen and scribbled. 'Bye, and thanks. Sounds good. You too. Bye.'

She looked up; Kirsty had gone, leaving tension behind her. Maybe it was time for a fresh start. Just look at those 'Likes' she'd had for her news.

Monday

To: <Sarah Knowles> Sarah.Knowles@townplanning.luton.gov.uk
Sender: Martin Thomas Martin.Thomas@townplanning.luton.gov.uk
Date: March 10th 2014 17:25
Subject: Town Planning World Meeting Notes Day 1

Sarah,

Sorry to be a bore at this late hour, but I need you to type up the fruits of my labour. Apols if they're a little on the rushed side, but I am sure your lovely fingers can transform them into stardust for me to present to the powers that be tomorrow morning. A little PowerPoint would be nice too. Email them when they're done. I don't need them until 9am.

Off out now to oil the wheels of local government.
Best - Martin
PS: Hope you're enjoying the NEC. Don't work too hard ;-)
Chief Planner
Luton Town Council
Working to keep Luton special

Text Message from: Sez
Kirsty, the boss has dropped me in it and I can't get the bloody laptop to boot! Any ideas? Call me!
Sxx

Sarah placed her phone onto the desk next to her laptop and looked through the Happy Inn's grimy window. The traffic on the main road was thinning now; the residents of Birmingham were tucked up in bed or curled up in front of their televisions, Labradors at their feet. She was still working. At nine o'clock. But then she wasn't actually working. No. The placement that had all started so well was heading for disaster. After two days tottering around following her charge, Luton's own planning supremo, Martin Thomas, she was now tasked with using a program she had never encountered before, and writing a presentation on a subject she knew next to nothing about.

She sighed and stared up at the ceiling, hoping for inspiration. Why had she described her year off in South East Asia as a master's degree in town planning? She went to the mini-bar to seek an answer. Having downed a few 'answers' the bar was soon empty except for a KitKat and a festering packet of nuts. She went downstairs, following the sounds of chattering and laughing.

The hotel's 'Flying Pig Pub' was full of relaxing aircrew, stressed almost-holiday-makers and the players of the conference: planners from all over the country, minor local politicians with an axe to grind, pushy pressure groups, and builders looking for loopholes.

She glanced around for her party but they'd either gone to bed or moved on elsewhere.

She sat by the bar and ordered orange juice with two shots of vodka: three might spoil the taste.

'Sarah? Well if it isn't Sarah Knowles – what are you doing here – pilot or planner?' She was confronted by a face from her past. Five foot six inches of lard, greasy quiff, dubious facial hair and a grubby shirt: Paul Miller, the ex-computer geek at school (and one time almost-stalker). He wasn't staring at her face.

She crossed her arms, wishing her top was less revealing, and almost toppled the bar stool. He grabbed her shoulder. 'Steady!'

Her eye's darted around the room. 'Why, Paul, what a blast from the past!'

He jumped into a seat opposite, his knees rubbing against hers. He waved to the bar man and pointing at her glass said, 'Drink, m'lady?'

'No, no, just a quick break, still working actually.'

'You didn't answer my question; are you at the conference?'

'Oh, yes. Er, I'm in planning. Luton Town Council. How about yourself?'

'Ah, methinks you failed to escape the Kingdom of *Loitone*.'

The barman came over. Paul ordered a pint of Stella.

'Sorry?' Sarah said. 'Kingdom of?'

'*Loitone,* fair Luton, from whence we hail.'

Sarah stepped down from the stool. 'I must go, computer problems and a deadline. Maybe tomorrow?'

At the mention of a computer, Paul shot upright, as though receiving a minor electric shock. 'Computer? Perhaps I can help you.'

Before Sarah could answer, he was heading to the door, leaving her to follow in his wake. 'What's your room number?' he called over his shoulder.

'Paul, I really don't—'

'No, it's fine. It's what I do for a living; rescuing damsels in IT distress!'

In her room, he crossed to the laptop and started tapping away. Sarah looked nervously for somewhere to sit, other than the edge of the bed. She remained standing, door handle within reach. It was soon apparent that she needn't have worried. For Paul, computers clearly had more sex-appeal than young women.

'Got it,' he cried. 'The password was 3$42nR. Right let's see … umm … you planneth!' He'd opened her scrappy PowerPoint presentation and was paging through it. 'Ummm, that's not right, AAP is Area Action Plan not Aluminium Access Products. And CIL that's Community—'

Sarah stood looking over his shoulder. 'Oh, Paul, you've saved my life, I'm *really* grateful. I don't know these things; look I just had a few scrappy notes to go on. My boss he just …'

Paul didn't seem to be listening. He pressed on translating jargon understandable only to planning nerds. Sarah sat down on the bed. She watched him typing, but the sound of the clicking keys mixed with the drinks had a soporific effect; she dozed off. She was awoken by a hand on her arm.

'All done.'

She shot upright and pulled herself back against the headboard, glancing at the clock. An hour had passed. Oh dear, here she was, on her own in a hotel room with a lecherous nerd. She now owed him a favour. She felt a little the worse for wear.

'Now, how about a night-cap?' Paul said, taking a seat on the end of the bed.

Sarah stood up, smoothing down her skirt. 'Oh, Paul, I'm really tired and I have to get up early in the morning.' She opened the door. 'Thanks again.'

'Well you know where I am if you need me. How about dinner tomorrow night? Get to catch up properly?'

She suppressed a grimace. 'I'll see. Martin might need me.'

Warworld Chat

Thor Dazguard: *Met a real babe last night*
Vargo the Destroyer: *Do tell. B-)*
Thor: *A laydee from Skool-daze*
Vargo: *Big jugs? ;-)*
Thor: *lol. Absolutely stacked ☺☺. Really tasty. Brunette.*
V cute ☺☺
Vargo: *Do I get an intro?*
Thor: *Dream on – she said I was a knight in shining armour!*
Vargo: *Sounds like you're in mate!*
Thor: *Hope so, sounded keen, said she wanted to keep in touch. Got some good inside info off her for work too. Dad's very happy.*
Vargo: *You smoothy. Pleased the old man too? Must've been good.*
Thor: *Cheers, I'll keep you posted.*
Anyway, to business; bunch of Orks incoming
Vargo: *I got 'em. On my command, unleash Hell!*

Wednesday

To: <Kirsty> Kgrove@bedfordshirewildlifetrust.org>
Sender: Sarah Knowles Sarah.Knowles2002@hotmail.com
Date: Wednesday March 12th 2014 20:00
Hi Kirsty,

How come you never answer the phone these days? Someone's having too much fun – you going to introduce me?

Wish I could say the same. The only interest I've got is a guy I met at the show – our old class mate. Keeps texting and friending me. I am grateful for his help at that conference, but he is a bit of a minger. Any ideas?
Sx

To: <Sarah Knowles> Sarah.Knowles@townplanning.luton.gov.uk
Sender: Martin Thomas Martin.Thomas@townplanning.luton.gov.uk
Date: Thursday March 13th 2014 1913
Subject: Re: Meeting Notes day 4
Sarah,

Sorry to do this to you again. Last set of notes attached. Bit of a summary of the week for the chaps on Monday. Just sprinkle them with your PowerPoint magic once again. I need them for Monday first thing. See you back in your new office at Luton HQ. With skills like yours we may be able to find something more permanent to reward your lovely endeavours.
Best - Martin
PS: Have a nice weekend! I'm off fishing with Lucilla.
Chief Planner
Luton Town Council
Working to keep Luton special

Sarah swore and opened the Word document. It was garbage and five times as long as the previous efforts. She wouldn't be able to decode all these abbreviations and acronyms. On this last night she'd hoped for some social life with the rest of the conference gang. She sighed.

A Skype contact request popped up with a message, *'PaulM92 Great to catch up on Monday. Let's link up!'*

That was fortuitous timing. Maybe the pain was best dealt with in one go.

Hi Paul, need your help. Can you come over? I'll make it worth your while. ;-)

She deleted the last sentence. That could spell disaster.

Coming right over. Donning suit of armour now.

She went to her case, pulled out a fleece jumper, swapped leggings for jeans and tied her hair back. She looked in the mirror, turning from side to side. Yep, she was looking maximally unsexy.

Cheap aftershave, followed by Paul, arrived in ten minutes. He had dressed for the occasion. Gone was the filthy shirt. He wore an almost clean white T-shirt and fresh jeans, wide leather belt constricting his belly. He smiled and pushed back his fringe. 'So what's the problem, fair damsel?'

'I'm sorry, Paul, it's the same as before. A big pile of poo from my boss. Needs decoding. I've got until Monday but I am away all weekend and …'

'Anywhere nice?'

Sarah crossed her fingers behind her back. 'Girly thing, you know.'

He sat in front of the laptop, paused and said, 'And what would the fair maiden be giving me in return?'

Sarah felt herself redden, 'Oh, Paul, I'll pay you of course. What's the hourly rate for this sort of thing?'

He pushed the wheeled chair back from the desk. 'I don't want that sort of payment.' His face was serious.

'Look, Paul, I like you, we go back a long time don't we? But just friends, yeah?'

'But you haven't even agreed to my friend request have you? You wouldn't want me to feel used, would you?'

'No, no. Sorry, I never really check Facebook.' She realised how implausible this was, given her lavish Facebook page. 'I just need this last favour, please?'

'And I want something from you.' The words curdled and rolled across the table. 'Don't worry, it isn't your body.'

Sarah exhaled loudly and sat on the edge of the bed.

'No need to look so relieved,' Paul said.

'No, of course not, it's just—'

Paul held up his hand. 'Simple favourette. The king begs that you be our eyes and ears at the council. Just in case we need them.'

'Your dad? Eyes and – look, Paul, it's just a temp assignment. I'll be gone in a week. I really don't—'

'They won't want to lose you, particularly once they get this great set of notes.' And with that he swung his chair around and got to work.

An hour later he left. As the door closed behind him, she realised she hadn't even asked what he did now.

Warworld Chat

Thor Dazguard:	*Blown out by snooty pants!* ☹
Vargo the Destroyer:	*Joking!*
Thor:	*Just want to be friends. Usual BS. All the same.*
Vargo:	*Shame. Let me have a shot at her ;-)*
Thor:	*lol. Piss off*
Vargo:	*Joke*
Thor:	*You'll never guess what I found on her laptop though*
Vargo:	*Do tell*
Thor:	*Sorry, my little secret. Could come in handy one day. Let's just say it makes good bedtime viewing.*
Vargo:	*Spoilsport. Heh, watch out! Orksville USA*
Thor:	*Got it covered! Let's splat em!*

2015

Sarah Knowles stared out from the boardroom over the expansive car park. The last year had been incredible: a permanent PA position to the boss, then evening study and strings pulled saw her become a junior planner. She was on the committee, albeit as a dogsbody, for the biggest project of 2015, the new North Fields Leisure Centre. What a change from that unemployed ex-backpacker. A flat of her own and meeting Mr Right would make her life complete.

She looked across the dark table at the projector, refreshments, white board and plush chairs awaiting important rear ends.

She spotted Sir Keith Bradbury of Bradbury Construction in the car park, stepping out of his Rolls Royce. Today they would hear the first of the pitches from five firms competing for the lucrative leisure centre project, and for once she had a modicum of professional power to wield.

A small yellow Lotus caught her eye, navigating the speed bumps carefully, like a Dinky toy being manoeuvred by a three-year-old. Not the usual builder's car. Not the usual sort of car in the council car park either. A moment later, the desk phone trilled.

'Hello.'

'You have a visitor, says you know him. Paul Miller?'

Sarah blanched. What could he want? God. 'OK, I'll be down.'

In the steel and glass atrium, a very different Paul Miller waited: sharp suited, with designer sunglasses pushed up over his stylishly cut hair. What had happened to him?

He stood up as she came in and kissed her lightly on the cheek. Before she had time to say anything, he said, 'Hi Sarah, I realise you're busy, just wanted a quick word.'

Sarah ushered him into a meeting area, taking position inside the door.

'It's a simple thing really. Remember when I helped you out last year?'

'Yes?'

'Eyes and ears? Remember?' Paul crossed behind Sarah and shut the door.

'Yes, of course but—'

'Small thing really. Dad would like to see the other bids before he presents ours on Monday. That's all.'

Sarah's jaw dropped and for a moment she was speechless. 'But, Paul, they're confidential! You know I can't …'

'Oh come on. No one would know it was you.'

'It's outrageous. I'd lose my job. I can't. I mean I'm grateful and all that and I don't mind giving you, gossip, you know that sort of thing, but—'

Paul was holding up his hand. He reached into a leather satchel, pulled out an iPad and started playing with it. 'I was afraid that you might renege on our bargain.'

'It was hardly that!'

'I took a few precautions. You might want to close the blinds.' He nodded towards the floor-to-ceiling glass that looked out onto the busy atrium.

Confused, she closed the blinds, and looked at the video playing on the iPad; a low quality, amateurish video, but one she recognised. She sat down. 'Where did you get that?'

'Amazing what people leave on their laptops.'

'Please, Paul. No.'

'These things have a habit of going viral. You know how it is. Particularly when they're posted on your Facebook site for all your friends and family to see. How is your mother by the way?'

Sarah gaped.

'Forgot to say. I changed your Facebook password. I'll leave it alone for now. You'll need a few days to get the bids together. I won't post this up until Monday. Well, not at all probably, as I am sure you'll assist us.'

'I think you should leave.'

'Don't worry, I need to go. You know, help Dad on the last touches. Earn my cash. Oh, and don't bother trying to guess the password. From what I remember IT was never your strong suit.' He reached the door and turned to her. 'Don't look so sad. A little clue, it's my alter ego. You probably could get, what, maybe nine guesses in before Monday?'

He walked out, leaving Sarah sitting at the table, head in hands.

Thursday

'Kirst, what the hell should I do? I'm screwed, I'll never get a reference even.'

'Being screwed is the issue methinks. What were you thinking of?' Kirsty said, not looking up from her PC.

'It was bloody Mark. I didn't even know he was filming. One of the reasons I dumped him, he was so sleazy. Can't you just leave that for a minute, Kirst – I'm having a crisis here!'

'Sorry, just job-hunting, something good has come up.'

'What with a headset on? C'mon, you're on Skype to your mystery bloke aren't you? Let me see—'

'Mind your own,' Kirsty said, hitting the power button.

'Oh, suit yourself. I'm having a crisis here.' Sarah stormed out of the room back to the lounge. On the table sat the little pen drive holding the copies of the bids. Just taking it home would get her sacked, let alone … She reached for the half-empty wine bottle. Less than a day and one way or another she would be making major adjustments in her life.

'Look, I'll see if anyone knows him, can wheedle it out of him. He's such a pig.' Kirsty came back in, her headset drooping around her neck. 'I'm sure he won't go through with it. What would that say about him? He's just winding you up.'

'Oh he'll go through with it. Nothing traced to him. No one will care where it came from anyway. I'll have to go and live in Thailand again.'

'Think they have the internet there too.'

'Thanks.'

Friday

The blue bar slowly crossed the screen, little brown manila folders jumping. Of course no one would see this happen, but she couldn't help checking that someone hadn't just crept up behind her, P45 in hand, flanked by burly security guards.

It was insurance, that was all. She had some ideas. Three tries a day and the site locked her out, that was all she had. What would an IT geek call himself? Norman Nerd? Gregory Geek?

The pen drive stopped flashing. She pulled it out and dropped it into her bag, stood up and headed for the door. Outside it was dark; the street lights illuminated trees swaying in the breeze. Crossing the car park, she saw something on her windscreen. Her pace quickened.

She knew what the envelope contained without even opening it, and was tempted to rip it up there and then, but instead yanked it off the glass as she opened her door.

'Sarah?'

It was Charles, her new boss. He'd appeared out of nowhere. She felt herself flush, grateful for the poor light.

'Everything all right?' he said, nodding in the direction of her windscreen.

'Oh, yes, fine. Just boxed someone in, that's all. You know, rude note.'

'That's not on. Do you want me to look at it?'

'No, no. Thanks anyway.'

'Big day tomorrow. Croftons, the penultimate bid—'

'Yes, sorry, must go. See you, Charles.' She climbed into the seat and slammed the car into reverse, slowing down as she saw the 10 MPH sign. A glance in her mirror showed Charles staring quizzically after her. *He must think I'm crazy.* Could she have acted any more suspiciously? When that inevitable leak enquiry happened, he was sure to remember this moment …

Saturday

'Come on, what d'you know about this guy?'

'We've been through this. School nerd everyone hated. Probably a pervert. Now rich and trendy, no doubt courtesy of his obnoxious pillar-of-the-community dad. Likes to steal private films from other people's computers and leave pornographic photos on their car windscreen—'

'OK, enough,' Kirsty said. 'What's his weakness? Could you strike back? Is he scared of his dad? Can you go to him?'

Sarah laughed. 'It was probably his idea. The guy was a total arse; I remember him at prize-giving, always pride of place whilst his son skulked around examining our breasts.'

'OK, then what are his hobbies? He must have had a friend of some sort. Come on, what "alter ego"?'

'Probably something computer related, you know gaming, that sort of thing. Certainly nothing involving girls or fresh air.'

'What … sort of gaming?' Kirsty put her cup of tea down on the kitchen table.

'Oh, I don't know. This is just speculation.' Sarah stood up. 'What's the latest, greatest thing? Whatever a nerd with the biggest graphics thing in town wants to parade. He's probably a space pirate or goblin or something.'

'Oh, I give up. I was just trying to help. Good luck.' Kirsty swept out of the room, leaving Sarah staring at the Facebook login screen, 'Invalid user name or password' written across it. Three more guesses and that was that.

Warworld Chat

Thor Dazguard:	*Snooty pants is about to take a fall!*
Vargo the Destroyer:	*Tell all?*
Thor:	*Almost hope she doesn't come up with the goods, then you will get to see the little home video.*
Vargo:	*Can't wait!*
Thor:	*lol. Still. Shame she's so stuck-up.*
Vargo:	*You never said who she was*
Thor:	*Oh, no one you know*
Vargo:	*Do tell*
Thor:	*You can be first to check her page. Try Sarah Knowles.*
Thor:	*Yo? Vargo – you there?*
Vargo:	*Soz, just got distracted. I'll check her out.*
Thor:	*Now?*
Vargo:	*Nah, business before pleasure and all that.*

Sunday, 7pm

Sarah sat in front of the screen, looking at a pad covered in crossed-out names. She had three goes for today and then that was it, she would be locked out until the same time tomorrow.

Kirsty stuck her head around the door. 'Try Thor Dazguard.'

'What?'

'Thor Dazguard.' She leant over the desk and wrote it amongst the scribbles on the pad.

'What the—'

'Just try it!'

Sarah typed the name into the password box.

Invalid User ID

'Without the space,' Kirsty said.

And then, her home page appeared. Sarah gasped and slumped back into her seat. 'Kirsty, I could kiss you! How on Earth did you …?'

'I think that will remain my little secret. So, you going to change it then? Go on!'

Sarah looked to the ceiling and steepled her fingers. 'Actually. No. I'm not. But I might need a little technical help from you …'

Monday, 9am

The meeting couldn't come quickly enough. Sarah paced the room, checking her watch, checking the window. Paul was teasing her, keeping her waiting. She smiled to herself, and then practised hiding it. She mustn't smile. Not yet.

Out of the corner of her eye she saw a flash of yellow blast into the car park, bounce over the speed bumps and screech to a halt in front of reception.

The desk phone rang and Sarah went down to reception, heart racing.

Paul was standing at the reception desk, tapping his fingers, his eyes darting around the room. He smiled thinly and held out his hand. Sarah ignored it and said, 'Follow me.' She headed back to the stairs before she had seen his reaction.

He caught up with her and grabbed her arm, quickly releasing it as two women came around the corner. Under his breath he said, 'Is this necessary, let's just have the info. No need for us to be seen together.'

Sarah said nothing, but swiped the access control at the top of the stairs, letting him follow her to a small meeting room.

'There it is,' she said, pointing to an all-too familiar laptop, sitting open on the table.

'What are you playing at? What's wrong with a pen drive?'

'Sorry, as you said, no good at IT.'

'Good job I've bloody got one,' he said, and sat at the computer. 'So where are the bids? Save me a bit of trouble, darling, and I'll get out of your hair.' He opened an Explorer window and waved at the screen.

'Oh, silly me. I can't remember,' Sarah said, sitting across the desk from him.

He looked up sharply. 'Oh, stop the games.'

'Or else what?'

'You know what! Eternal Facebook shame. You never know, you might even make the tabloids.'

'You realise that attempting to blackmail a government worker is a criminal offence?'

Paul stood up and walked to the door. 'You *will* regret this. I am going to enjoy posting this filth up.'

Sarah leant across and, taking the laptop, started typing. Paul hesitated by the door, watching her. 'What exactly are you doing?'

'Oh, just emailing the video of your threats somewhere safe. By the way I changed my Facebook password, *Thor.*'

Paul's face turned ashen. 'You bitch! How on earth?'

'Shut the door and sit down.'

A look of confusion flashed across Paul's face. He complied.

'I'm going to call in my boss now and you will tell him formally that you have decided not to bid on the leisure centre. After that I will never see nor hear of you again.' She folded up the laptop and headed to the door. 'Don't go anywhere.'

She allowed herself a small smile in his direction.

Epilogue

Warworld Chat

Thor Dazguard:	*Last battle for me for a while.* ☹
Vargo the Destroyer:	*Why?*
Thor:	*Bit of a change of career direction. Planning some time away from computers and family.*
Vargo:	*Sorry to hear it. Miss your hammer.*
Thor:	*lol. I'll be back. Did you ever check out that Sarah?*
Vargo:	*Nah, forgot. Still like to see the vid though.*
Thor:	*Best not. Wouldn't be fair.*
Vargo:	*Oh well, if this is the end, let's make it a good one. I'm in position!*
Thor:	*Let's go!*

Sunset – Alison May

'Look at the sunset!'

I'm sitting on a bench. I look to where you're pointing and nod. It's a sunset. It's going behind some fields, which have grass on them, and sheep. It's the sort of scene they have in books.

'Isn't it beautiful?' You're genuinely enthused. It's one of your oddities, the way you get excited by the beauty of everyday things. Or maybe it's one of my oddities that I don't. It's one of the ways you make me think I could become better. A couple walk past us. They're being idly trailed by a bored-looking dog. They nod a greeting.

I watch you for a moment. You're wearing a pink waterproof over a flippy wafty summer dress, and your blonde hair is twisted up in an artfully messy pile on top of your head. You're exquisite. I glance at my chipped nail varnish, and wonder what you see in me. Boobs too small, feet too big, hair too frizzy – I can only ever be beautiful when you look at me.

I pull my phone out of my pocket. I could tweet a picture of the sunset; it would be a form of participation in the moment. Without my brain engaging, my fingers open the Facebook app instead. I look to see if she's responded to your comment. No notification. I swipe and thumb to my friend list and scroll down past the As and Bs to find her name. Bobbi, Carl, Ceri, Cynthia. I scroll back up. No Cara.

'That's weird.'

'What?' You turn towards me and sigh. 'Phone away!'

'Sorry.' I stuff it back in my pocket. 'What do you want to do now?'

You move in front of me wiggling your hips into the space between my knees. You giggle. 'Back to the hotel?'

'Ok.' I blink.

For a second it feels like something's shifting underneath me. All my senses feel wrong, like they're giving my brain information it can't process. I'm still outside, but I'm in a street, not a park. There's no sunset. It's already dark. And I'm cold. It only lasts a second. I blink.

Back at the hotel, you decide to have a shower. I sit on the bed and listen to you singing Taylor Swift to yourself under the rushing water. I get my phone back out and look at Facebook again. She still hasn't commented.

My status is still there. I'm eternally somewhere out there in the data cloud, enjoying my weekend by the sea. You've commented that it's 'brill' to be here too. I've liked your comment. She hasn't. I feel a sort of tightness across my chest. She must have seen it. She must look. Nobody would simply let you go.

I flick back to my friend list, and scroll down. She's not there. Cow. She must have unfriended me. I scroll back to the search box and type in her name. It's an unusual name and there are only eight matches: six in America, one in New Zealand and one in Northern Ireland. None of them are her. Has she blocked me altogether?

I wonder if her profile's public. I switch back to the homescreen and google her name. I swipe through the first few pages of results. Lots of Caras. Caras on census records. Caras in graduating classes. Caras in local newpapers. One notable Cara imprisoned after helping her brother break out of jail. Still, none of them are her.

You get out of the shower and pad into the bedroom, towel wrapped around you, practically going all the way around your tiny frame twice. You pick your hairbrush from the pile of detritus you've left scattered around the room's only chair and start alternating between brushing your hair and using it as a dummy microphone for your continued singing.

'Mel.'

You stop singing and grin at me. 'Sorry. I'll act like a grown-up.'

'No.' It's really not that. 'It's Cara.'

You put the hairbrush down altogether this time, and when you speak it sounds wary. 'What about her?'

'She's disappeared.'

'What do you mean?'

I swallow. I need to find a tone of voice that will make you take this seriously. 'Cara's disappeared.'

'What? When?' You rummage for your phone in the bottom of your handbag. 'How do you know? Did someone call?'

I'm confused. 'No. No. Not like that. She's disappeared off Facebook.'

You stop. 'Facebook?'

I nod. 'Not just Facebook. I can't find her when I google either.'

You sit down at my feet, lean towards me and wrap your hands around mine. 'Why were you googling her?'

'Because I thought she'd blocked me on Facebook.'

'And you care about that, why?'

'It's rude.' I sound truculent now, like a child. This is always how it goes. You skip about like an eight-year-old who's had too many jelly worms, and then it comes to moments like this and it's absolutely clear that I'm the sulky teenager in the relationship and you're the long-suffering adult. You're more fun and more sensible than me all at the same time. You make me understand what people mean when they say things feel too good to be true.

You push my hair out of my face and wriggle to try to keep your towel up over your boobs. 'Why does it matter whether my ex-girlfriend is friends with you on Facebook? Being mates with your own ex is weird enough.'

'You said you weren't mates with her?' My intonation's rising and the words rush out over one another.

'I'm not.' You don't sound cross, just resigned. It's not my fault. It's yours really for being so far out of my league.

'It's not just Facebook though. She's vanished. She's nowhere on the internet. Look.' I get my phone out and search for her twittername. Nothing. I repeat my google search. Nothing.

You shrug. 'So she's deleted some accounts?' You lift the phone out of my hands. 'That might not be such a bad idea, all round. A bit of real-life virtual-life balance?'

'You don't understand!' I can hear the slight shriek in my own voice. I can hear how I'm sounding. I'm not going to be like that. Being with you's going to make that hole in the middle of me go away. I put a smile on. 'You're probably right. It's not our problem anyway.'

You grin. Carefree you is coming back. 'Right. Now, I thought this was supposed to be a dirty weekend?' You crawl up the bed so that you're straddling me, and you let your towel fall away from your breasts. You lean towards me, and I tilt my head to kiss you. I close my eyes.

I'm in the other place again. It's a street, a normal sort of residential street. I'm standing outside a particular house, a plain-looking semi-detached. I walk towards it. I don't know why I walk towards it, but somehow I know that I always do.

I open my eyes. I'm sitting on the park bench watching the sun set over the field of sheep.

'Isn't it beautiful?'

You're smiling at me. You're here. I'm here. This is wrong. 'Have we been here before?'

You look blank.

'We have. We've been here before.' I look around. 'There was a couple walking a dog.'

'Don't think so.'

But there was. I look around again. There isn't now.

You step away from me gazing at the setting sun. I get my phone out to see if she's responded to your comment, and I get another flash. It's like de ja vu, but more so, not just having done this before, but knowing what I'm going to do next before I've thought of doing it. I search my friend list, and then google. Nothing. I flick to my phone contacts, and scroll to the 'C's. Nothing again. Actually, less than nothing. No Cara, but no Carl either. I scroll down further. Dad's there, but no Mum. I hold my breath and my thumb slides back up the 'M's. You're still there.

I look up towards the falling sun. You're still here. I breathe.

'This is weird.'

'What?'

'Loads of people have disappeared off my phone.'

You shrug. 'Shall we go back to the hotel?'

I blink.

We're in the hotel room. I can hear you in the shower. I get my phone out and check again. The list's getting shorter.

You come out of the shower.

'It's not just Cara.'

'What?'

'Nearly all my contacts have disappeared. People are disappearing.'

You pause in front of the mirror striking a pop star pose with your hairbrush.

'Probably something wrong with your phone.'

'But they're not on Facebook anymore either.'

You put the hairbrush down. 'Who?'

'Cara. Carl. Everyone. People are disappearing.'

'From your phone?'

'No! Yes!' I stop for a second. 'I don't know.'

'Your contacts sync to Facebook. If that's playing up it'll probably mess your contact list up too.'

I nod.

'Good. Now, why were you looking for my ex-girlfriend anyway?'

I shrug. 'I thought she'd unfriended me.'

You come over to the bed and push my hair out of my face. You have to wriggle to keep your towel over your boobs, and I feel like I've seen you do it before.

'Being mates with your own ex is weird enough,' you say.

I think of you being mates with her and my stomach contracts. I don't question it though. I know what you'll say anyhow. I try to put a smile on. 'You're probably right.'

You grin. Carefree you is coming back, but it makes me shiver. More de ja vu.

'You're going to kiss me now, aren't you?'

You laugh. 'I thought I might. Yeah.'

I try to breathe and remember that I enjoy you. I love you. A year ago I would have done anything to have you here. Being with you is like being in heaven, a fragile heaven that I could break in a moment. You lean towards me, and I ignore the unease reaching down my gut. I tilt my head to kiss you. I close my eyes.

Things shift again. I'm right outside the house now. I've moved up the driveway and round the back of the building to the French windows. It's dark inside, and I think it must be late at night. I know where I am. I know whose house this is. I could get closer. Close enough to touch you. I reach for the door handle. It's not locked.

I open my eyes. The bench. The fields. The sunset. You. But this time I remember. It's not a just a feeling. I absolutely know that we have been here before. Only it's different. Something's missing. Everything seems a little bit less clear.

You tell me that the sunset's beautiful, but I'm not listening. I've already got my phone out. I flick to my contacts. Only you.

Facebook – the same. Email – the same. Everyone's gone. Everyone but you. Me and you.

'What's happening?' There's a note of panic in my voice.

'We're looking at the sunset.'

'Where is everyone?'

'What do you mean?'

I listen for a second. There's no sound. No traffic moving in the distance. No yells of chatter from other parts of the park. I look around. No couple walking a bored-looking dog. No sheep in the fields.

'There's only me and you here.' But that's not quite right. 'There's only me and you anywhere.'

You step towards me tilting your head to one side. 'Isn't that what you wanted?'

It's all I ever wanted. I nod. Your lips smile and your face moves towards me. I tilt my head to kiss you. I start to close my eyes and stop. I shove you. Hard. Pushing you away.

'No! It's when I close my eyes.'

'What?'

'That's when it happens.'

'When what happens?'

I can't think. I can't work it out. We're here, in a park on a bench, but that's not where we should be. I try to remember how we got here. We were at the hotel. And then? I can't fill in the gaps. I try to go backwards. Before we were at the hotel we were? We were here.

You're looking at me. Your face is jammed full of concern, waiting for me to explain.

'It's like we jump. I close my eyes and then we jump, from here to the hotel and then back here.'

'What hotel?'

I try to remember but it's not there.

'I don't know.' I'm still clasping my phone in my hand. I hold it up. 'And everyone's disappeared.'

'Who?'

'Everyone. My parents. My brother.' I stop, trying to think who else. 'Cara.'

Your face changes. The concern is gone. Everything's gone. You're blank, and when you talk it's not your voice at all. You're a shell hiding something much much worse. 'Do you remember when Cara disappeared?'

I try to sift through the memories. 'We were here.'

'No.'

'We were. You were looking at the sunset. You were happy.' Those moments with you when you're full of joy. They're my heaven.

'It was before then. Where were you?'

I can't think. I still can't see anything before here and now.

'Close your eyes.'

I shake my head.

You yell. 'Close them.'

It happens again, but this time I'm inside the house. A kitchen. Your kitchen. Her kitchen. There's someone coming. I grab the nearest thing I can reach to protect myself. I've been here before. I've done these things before.

It's her. Cara. She walks up to the fridge without putting the light on, bends down, pulls out a bottle, turns so she's facing me and then screams. I have to make the scream stop. That's all it is. I don't want to hurt her. I have to do what I do. It's what I did before. It's what I do every time. It's not even a choice anymore.

Then you come. You run down the stairs and into the room. You must have heard the scream and you see me there and you see her on the floor and for a second I think you're going to scream too, but you don't. You're silent. You don't move or speak or shout. You just stand there and stare. And for a second it's just you and me, and she's not here anymore. It's everything I wanted. It's what you wanted too, isn't it? Only, you're staring at my hands which are wet and warm with her blood. I want to make the whole scene go away. I close my eyes.

I open my eyes. I'm on the bench, but everything else is empty. Not black or grey, just empty. There's a half-circle of orange sun low in the distance and there's you.

'When did Cara disappear?'

'When I made her disappear.'

'And then what happened?'

'I don't remember.'

You shake your head, only it's still not you. It's something inside your face, but it's not happy or angry or sexy. It's just here, and when it talks it's like the words come hissing straight into my brain. 'You ran away. You vanished. And eight months later you jumped in front of a train. Did you think that meant you couldn't be punished?'

I don't remember. I remember the hotel room. I remember you dancing and singing wrapped in your towel. That was real. What's happening now is something else.

'You're thinking this isn't real.'

'I was in heaven.'

'No.' The thing that was never really you shakes its head. 'Not heaven.'

Tea and Tittle-Tattle – Tana Durham

'You will never believe what I just heard,' Mary said, dumping her bags next to Ruth Johnston's table. 'I can't tell you though.'

Ruth arched her shaped brows, her Choc-nut Cookie halfway to her filler-enhanced lips. 'Tell me what?'

Mary hovered, eyeing the thick chocolate-covered biscuit. *What I'd do for one of those. Ooh and those meringues look good.*

'Umm … no. I can't. I promised.'

Ruth disliked her colleague. She thought her silly and unattractive. However, she did enjoy a titillating morsel of gossip.

'Sit down,' she purred, as she poured tea into an extra cup. 'Take the weight off. Try an orange and ginger flapjack.'

'How kind,' Mary said, as she flopped onto a chair. 'I am a bit peckish.'

Ruth watched with distaste as Mary tucked in. 'What were you going to tell me?'

'I really can't say. Interesting though.'

Ruth waved the plate temptingly under Mary's nose. 'Go on. The Melting Moments are divine. You can tell me. I won't tell a soul.'

Mary looked at her doubtfully as she popped the buttery biscuit into her mouth. She was sure Ruth had told everyone at work about her little problem. Otherwise why did everyone slip the word 'electrolysis' into conversations with her, even when chatting about the weather?

'I'd better not.'

She's harder to crack than I imagined she'd be, Ruth thought. Out loud she said, 'OK … I'm not really interested anyway. Have a Cherry Oaty.'

She smiled sweetly at her colleague. Perhaps flattery would work. 'The treatment is helping, Mary. Only a few stray hairs across the top lip and in front of your ears now. Met anyone interesting in the waiting room?'

Mary glared at her. 'No I have not!'

Mmm this is not going well. And she's scoffed all the best cookies. I'm going to have to divert her attention from that last Melting Moment. Ruth looked around the café and said brightly, 'Getting a bit tired looking in here. Mock Tudor has had its day don't you think?'

Mary merely sniffed.

Undaunted, Ruth continued, 'All the trendy places are in light ash, lime and French navy nowadays. I'm thinking of doing my kitchen in those colours.'

Mary took the bait. '*We're* planning a kitchen extension. Our decorator tells me pink is the new lime.'

'Sounds very modern. Are you using René? He did some work for me when John was in the Far East. I call it Louis 14th style. He was a hoot. Such stories!' She leant forward confidentially. 'Kept me entertained, I can tell you.'

Mary perked up. This was more like it. *'Go on.'*

'Don't say anything, but he brought in a team to *deep clean* the Lady Mayor's house before he could *start* on the decorating.'

'No! And she speaks so nicely.'

'That's no guarantee of high standards is it? Fleas and mice everywhere apparently.'

'You're kidding!'

'Better still, you know the woman who owns the boutique on the corner of Market Place? Well she's a he and he's got a pretty wife at home.'

'Really? Well he's very glamorous. I'd never have known. I just put the voice down to a twenty-a-day habit. I won't let him zip me into dresses any more.'

'No need to worry, dear. You're not his type. Come on. Now you. I've told two tasty morsels. You tell me your titbit.'

'Well, I don't like to gossip as you know, but if you promise not to tell a soul …?'

Ruth nodded eagerly. 'Cross my heart.'

'Well … René was telling me about this client. Not her name obviously 'cos she's in our line of work. Apparently she insisted on him doing up her bedroom like a tart's boudoir. Drapes, flounces and mirrors everywhere, even on the ceiling. God knows what her husband thought when he got back from abroad. Maybe he liked it. Apparently he keeps interesting company on his trips to Thailand. Anyway she was so pleased with René's work she wanted to give him a special bonus. Of the personal kind! Well, as he swings both ways he wasn't going to refuse was he? He told me she did such a good job he felt like taking some money off the bill.' Mary cackled and gave Ruth's arm a playful slap. 'He didn't of course. Now you keep that under your hat. I wouldn't want René getting into trouble.'

Fixing a smile on her face, which is hard when you're speaking through gritted teeth, Ruth said, 'You can be sure of that. But I'd change my decorator if I were you. René is a disgraceful old gossip. Share your shaving tips with him and it will be round the town in no time.'

The Changeling – Polly Robinson

'What are these things?' Sarah asks, picking up a pinch of pointy green stick-like things the size of hundreds and thousands.

John stares, his eyes wide in amazement. 'They're tiny! How on earth did you spot them?'

He's right; mortals rarely see faerie teeth.

The collective gasp from the fae sounds like a breath of wind; Alemin flies, his wings on fire, to the faerie court.

'Mortals! Mortals!' he wheezes. 'Found the teeth.'

The faerie queen grins, her mouth glittering greenly. 'Mark her! We'll take the child.'

The fae pack their string pockets. They have nectar to feed the mortal babe and keep it quiet when they put the changeling in its place. The faerie court, the tannafae, wants a blue-eyed, blonde-haired boy child to pet, cosset and tease … to keep for the solstice. The fae hunters head for the land of mortals.

'This way.' Alemin leads as they leave the magical meadow-scented realm. They pass through the hawthorn to the world of mortals. Alemin hates the green stained teeth; he rubs a tooth-cleansing twig over his own to freshen his mouth. He hears them chattering and jittering behind him; he sees squirrels leap up trees, rabbits disappear down holes. There are snuffles and scuffles. Twigs snap. He was born into fae. Why is he different? Why can't he feel a part of them? Alemin glances up through the dappled canopy, mottled sunshine picks out bright spikily waxed hair, disproportionately large knuckled hands, thin fingers, tapered nails. He is aware of them scraping the unmistakeable fae marks in moss and on tree bark. Coal black faerie eyes glitter; the fae sneer at the creatures scattering before them.

At Alemin's raised hand the fae hunters quieten and move swiftly, silently in shoes of scuffed moleskin. Alemin carries a poor sickly little mite, blue-eyed and blonde-haired, a faerie baby, the one his family call the good-for-nothing, the changeling. He does not like it, what he is about to do, but it must be done. He, Alemin, must be elevated to the position of tannafae and from there to faepeer. He has little choice until he can win enough favour to become tannafae. They reach the archaic ridgeway and work along it. There, in front of them, appears the isolated cottage. Alemin makes a wide sweep with his arm and the fae blend into the gorse and bracken on the hillside. Not a sound is made.

Alemin sees Sarah pegging out washing. She is their target mother; the mortal who picked up the faerie teeth. Alemin and the others enter the farmworker's cottage. They snatch Sarah's child from the cradle and Alemin deposits the faerie changeling. Without a backward glance, the fae leave. Alemin stops outside the window to see what Sarah will do. She peels potatoes for dinner, cries over onions, then she moves to the cradle. Alemin sees her tilt her head to the side as if puzzled. He stiffens. Will she realise? No. Trick of the light. She tucks the blankets around the tiny child. She smiles fondly at the baby who grizzles in his sleep.

The tannafae coo over the tiny new mortal, delighted with the blue eyes and blonde hair. They pinch it to make it cry, then pick it up and fuss it. Alemin sees they love the novelty. He feels sick. They chuck it under its chin to receive a gummy smile. They feed it on nectar, giggling as it becomes drunk and starts to hiccup. Alemin looks away.

The faerie queen smiles and nods her head graciously. She is pleased with Alemin.

He shivers as he thinks about the solstice, the blood-tithe. Before the last solstice he talked with his father.

'Why do we need mortal blood?'

'Because otherwise it would have to be fae blood.'

'But it is fae blood if we give away our weak and feeble to get mortals'

'That's not how she sees it. The fae hunters search for the mortals who find faerie teeth. It has been so for centuries.'

'They are away from their families for months. What's the good of that? There has to be a better way.'

'You are a great hunter, Alemin; you have the knack of spotting teeth finders and marking them for the blood-tithe.'

'But there must be a better way.'

'Find it, my son. Get into court. Become a tannafae. With good fortune you could be nominated a faeseer, then you'll make your mark.'

Alemin knows he has pleased the faerie queen. He will soon join the tannafae.

At the faerie court, the tannafae fun lasts until the babe is so hungry it won't stop crying and doesn't smile any more. They tire of sticking it with pins to make it scream louder. Now the sacrifice is made, the blood-tithe gathered. They put the limp bloodless body on the bones of others in the northern cave; the babe will die of cold, blood poisoning and anaemia.

Another half dozen and the fae will be safe until winter solstice.

The Decision – Kevin Brooke

Soon it will be my turn to make the decision. I've seen over the last few weeks how difficult it is for some and how they agonise and deliberate. It won't be like that for me, however – I've seen how it works, and when the time comes, I'll know what to do.

Things are different now, of course they are; dying is like that – it changes everything. But even so I'm sure I'll be okay. Why else would I have been given this job, if it weren't as proof of my integrity when I was alive?

There was no instruction, no training course as such. I did see the previous guy on what turned out to be his last day. I remember watching him telling the passengers which stop was theirs and then, when the time was right, getting off the train himself. He seemed like a good man, just like me. He even received a round of applause when he left the carriage for the last time. It was quite moving. I expect it will be similar when it's my turn.

My approach is a bit different from his. I don't tell the passengers which stop is which – instead I let them make their own choice. I'm a believer in fate you see; always have been. I think it's best to allow a simple game of chance to make the decision for them.

'Where are we going?' is usually their first question as I welcome them aboard.

'You'll be alright,' I say. It isn't a complete lie – some of them will be.

'I didn't get the chance to say goodbye,' some cry – particularly those involved in sudden accidents or those who just didn't see it coming.

'Don't worry, you'll get another chance,' I say, even though I have no idea whether they will or not. What's it to me anyway? I'm not there to comfort them. It's too late for that. The carriage fills quickly – the routine is always the same. The more people who arrive, the harder it is for me to move amongst the crowd and speak to them all – well that's my excuse anyway. They tell me their names sometimes: Erica, Brian, Peter, Susan or whatever. They tell me what job they have or about their families. I don't really listen, to be honest. Then the panic sets in and someone starts to scream as they realise where they are and what has happened to them.

You have to get used to that. I've found the best way around it is to put my hands over my ears to block out the noise. The one bit of good news I always tell those close by me is that for some of them it will soon be over; the first stop is never far away. This doesn't seem to help; in fact, for some, it seems to makes it worse somehow.

The train slows down.

'It's time to make a choice,' I shout, as we reach the first station of two. For the first time the doors open from the inside. People look at me with pleading expressions.

'Look inside yourself,' I say. 'Make your decision.'

There is nothing more I need to say. I look around the carriage; guilt wells up in some of the faces, as if they know instinctively that this is their stop. Others aren't so sure, but a few of them get off anyway, and others follow, but not all of them.

The train pulls away and I look through the back window at those passengers who alighted, some still standing on the platform. Many appear confused and look at each other for guidance. Then, as the gloom descends around them, a few of them accept their destiny and begin to move away. I watch them, heads bowed, dragging themselves towards the blackened steps and the darkness below.

Some of the others remain motionless on the platform – the ones who do not appear weighed down with the shame of their lives. They realise their mistake and try to get back on the train, but they can't. Once they've left the carriage there's no coming back.

The train moves away from the station – the frightened, desperate expressions of the innocent we've left behind fading into the distance. I always stop looking at this point. I made the mistake of watching what happened next the first time – the flames engulfing them, the agony in their faces too much to bear a second time.

I feel guilty. I always feel guilty for a moment or two but not for long. It's not my fault is it? I didn't force them to get off, did I? Fate has decided their lot and that is just the way it is. You don't always get what you deserve in life, or in death. I'm just glad that when the time comes I'll know which stop is which. I'll be alright. I won't make the same mistake as them, and anyway I know I'm a good man – why else would they have given me this job?

I turn and look back into the carriage at those who are left.

'The rest of you will be okay,' I tell them. It's the first complete truth I've spoken since the start of the journey.

I can see the evil and the hatred in some of them – those with the smug faces who know they've got away with it. Instead of being consigned to an eternity of pain, they will receive a comfort they simply do not deserve; but like I said before, that's just the way it is.

This is how the journey goes every day and how it has been since I became this person, this transporter of souls as they make the transition. Every day these frightened and bewildered looking people get on my train at regular intervals, appearing as if out of nowhere. Then we go through the same old routine of the two stations at the end of the line where they make their fateful decision. Then the train reverses and the process repeats itself.

Nothing has changed; nothing has altered in any way – until today that is. Today my train, instead of reversing to the start after the second set of passengers alights, continues in the same direction.

I'm not worried, to begin with anyway. Then the speed of the train increases. Faster and faster it goes, as though it will never stop.

I tense my body, expecting the carriage to crash into something at any moment, but instead there is nothing, nothing except the flashes and images in my mind of the last few weeks and my time as a transporter.

The smiling faces come first – those I've helped get off at the right stop. They seem content and at peace, but not for long. The faces change; their features contort into something terrifying. It's my turn to be scared now, as something inside me screams, telling me that I should have helped them more, made it easier for them to make the right decision.

I'll change – I will. From now on you'll see a different me. I'll let the passengers know which stop is theirs. I'll be an even better man than I've been before. Don't you worry about that; I've learnt my lesson.

And then in an instant the faces in my mind have disappeared, hopefully forever.

I'm on a platform now, with the train next to me. I try to open the door but it won't budge. I look around expecting to see others nearby who can tell me where I am, but there is no one; just me.

I look through the train window. It's strange to see the carriage from the outside. There are a few people scattered around. In the background a man is talking to the passengers, reassuring and comforting them. I know instantly who he is; it can be no other. He is the new transporter – my replacement.

But where am I?

The light around me begins to fade and, as the temperature increases, I turn to see a set of darkened steps. This can't be right though, can it? I'm in the wrong place and anyway I know how this works – this was supposed to be MY decision. I knew which stop was mine and I knew where I had to get off. Something must be wrong.

I'm a good man, I know I am. I may have made a few mistakes in my life and then in death, but who hasn't? This just isn't right! I said I'd change. I said I'd be an even better man from now on, but why is no one listening?

I look up to see the train moving away from me. I sink to my knees and shut my eyes. Then everything makes sense. This isn't about fate after all. I was given a chance to demonstrate my worth when I was on the train – one last chance to prove my value, and I've ruined it.

There is nothing now, except for the heat of the flames behind me. I can't bear to look, but I know that the fire is coming ever closer. I feel its merciless breath on my arms, shoulders and neck.

My eternity of pain has begun.

The Game – Andy Kirk

Tara immediately fell in love with it – Belsbarc, that is, the holiday cottage we'd rented for the week.

'Steve, it's fabulous,' she said, her eyes scanning the profusion of colours in the garden. I couldn't deny its splendour, especially on such a beautiful summer's day. 'Come on, let's take a look inside,' Tara said excitedly, pushing open the gate and making her way to the front door.

I paused at the gate and looked at the short flagstone path, grass growing in the gaps, its borders crowded with peonies and poppies. It enticed me towards the trellised porch encircled by honeysuckle, its sweet fragrance delicately scenting the air, and the weathered wooden door.

To the left of the door was a small tree; its branches brushed against the white-washed brickwork of the cottage. Beneath it stood an old bench which, although even more weather-beaten than the front door, perfectly complemented its surroundings.

Tara had already reached the door and inserted the key. Slowly, she turned the handle and pushed. The door wouldn't budge.

'Give it a kick,' I said.

She glanced at me disapprovingly and then, twisting the handle again, applied shoulder pressure. The door creaked, in typical horror movie fashion, as it swung open. Musty air rushed out, as though trying to escape the confines of the room in which it had been trapped since its last occupancy.

We stepped into a small room, no more than twelve-foot square. The focal point was a huge open fire place. We wouldn't be using it – it was much too warm for that, but we could easily imagine how cosy it would be with a fire roaring on a frosty night.

Belsbarc was a warm and welcoming little cottage, and we soon settled in. We decided to stay in on that first evening. A nice meal was planned: a thick rump streak, mushrooms, fries and pepper sauce, accompanied by the obligatory glass or two of Merlot or Shiraz. Whilst hunting for wine glasses I found the box. I was pleasantly surprised, and I knew Tara would love it.

'Guess what's in here?' I said, holding up the box.

Curled up on the settee, Tara lowered her book. 'I give in,' she said in a hushed breath. 'What is it?'

'It's the most amazing *Scrabble* board you've ever seen! Hand-crafted.'

'Really?' She folded the corner of the page and closed the book. *Scrabble* was a favourite of hers, and she was dangerously good.

I sat down and pulled the heavy oak coffee table towards us; it screeched across the quarry tiled floor. I slid the game out of the box. The board and trays were made of solid oak which had been naturally stained and hand-painted. The tile bag was fine quality leather with a golden draw string. I pulled it open and emptied out the oak tiles, which clattered onto the board. Each letter and number had been meticulously scribed.

Tara smiled. 'It's been yonks since I've had a game. I challenge you … the loser makes dinner.'

'Okay, you're on. I'll have my steak medium-rare, please,' I added with a wink.

'You actually think you're going to win?' She rolled her eyes.

'I feel lucky,' I replied, putting the tiles back into the bag. 'You get the drinks and I'll set this up.'

Tara disappeared into the kitchen and quickly re-appeared with two large glasses of wine and a bag of nuts.

'Something to nibble on whilst we play,' she said, shaking the nuts with a grin.

'Good idea.' I shook the tile bag. 'And now, let the game commence.'

I studied my letters. *Too many vowels and not enough consonants*, I mused. I could only see a couple of small words; I plumped for *tan.* 'Double-word score – six points.'

Tara giggled. 'Thank you, kind sir.'

'What for?' I asked, replenishing my supply of letters.

'That *t* which you very nicely placed for me means I get to make a great word – and one with an amazing score, too!' She placed all her tiles on the board. 'There. *Trainers*, triple-word score, twenty-seven points, thank you very much!'

'Not bad,' I huffed.

'Not bad at all, especially as I also get fifty point's bonus for using all my letters in one go.'

'What? Seventy-seven points on your first go?' I shook my head in disbelief. 'Well, it's not how you start, it's how you finish that counts!' I said, smiling.

It was my turn. '*Spilt*,' I said. 'See, I'm getting better – nine points.' I glanced away for a second, and the unexpected expletive caught me by surprise.

'Oh shit!' Tara raged.

My head automatically snapped up. The red river of wine was already flowing over my side of the table.

'I didn't go anywhere near it! The glass just tipped on its own!' Tara said as she made her way into the kitchen. She ran back into the lounge with two tea towels and threw one at me; we mopped up. 'I swear I didn't touch the glass, it just … well, it kinda tipped over on its own.' She frowned.

'Don't be silly, the table's uneven, that's all,' I said, pushing on it to demonstrate. 'See? Wobbly as hell.'

'Oh right.' She didn't look convinced.

With the wine cleaned up and the board reset, we were ready to continue our game. It was Tara's turn.

'*Cane*,' she said. 'Seven points.' She placed the tiles neatly in position.

I looked at my letters – I was still struggling. 'The best I can do is … *rain*,' I muttered.

'Good timing,' she quipped.

'What do you mean?' She nodded towards the window behind me. I turned to see large drops of rain splattering on the glass. 'Where the hell did those clouds come from? It was lovely when we started playing.'

'Maybe the board's cursed.'

'Very funny,' I said, sticking my tongue out. 'Go on – it's your turn.'

'Twenty-eight points, please,' she said with a huge smile, placing her letters to form *choked*.

'You jammy so-and-so.' I threw a handful of nuts into my mouth.

'It's all skill.' She marked the points on the pad.

Before I could play my next word I had a strange constricted feeling in my throat. I started to cough and splutter. I couldn't breathe. I stood up and staggered forward.

Jumping to her feet, Tara grabbed me and slapped me on the back. 'Steve? What's the matter?'

I had no way of answering, and now my consciousness was sinking fast. I dropped to all fours, my knuckles white against the hard floor. My shoulders hunched forward and my chest heaved as I strove vainly to force air into my lungs.

Tara threw her arms around my waist and, in one smooth movement, thrust her clenched fists hard up into my stomach. After several such Heimlich manoeuvres, the pressure on my throat started to ease. Finally, I could breathe again. I sucked in huge gulps of air, my blurred vision clearing as the oxygen reached my blood. I pushed myself to my feet.

'Are you alright?' Tara asked, her eyes sharp with concern.

'Yeah, must have choked on the nuts.' But it hadn't felt like choking … it felt … well … strange.

Tara had gone pale with shock. I didn't want to upset her anymore, so I forced the ridiculous thoughts to the back of my mind. 'That'll teach me to put too many nuts into my gob in one go,' I said, hoping to raise a smile.

She didn't smile, but frowned. 'Don't you think it's a bit weird though?'

'Weird? Why?' I asked, even though I knew exactly what she was getting at.

'The way things happen after words are placed on the *Scrabble* board.'

'It's just coincidence,' I said, trying to convince myself as much as Tara.

'But when you put *spilt* down …'

I didn't let her finish the sentence. I shook my head. 'No, come on … you're letting your imagination run away with you.'

'You're probably right.' Tara sat down. 'But … I don't think I want to play anymore.'

'Don't be silly, it's just coincidence.'

She still looked doubtful.

'Look, I'll prove it.' I picked up some of my tiles, contemplated the word *cane* and placed my letters above the *e* to form *explode.*

Tara sat silently looking around, holding her breath as though waiting for something to happen. Silence echoed around the room. She breathed a sigh of relief.

The relief, however, was short-lived. A bright flash of light illuminated the kitchen, and then came a deafening explosion. Splinters of wood, tiles and crockery scattered around the room, ricocheting off the walls, followed by a maelstrom of air currents. I clambered over to Tara and shielded her with my body from the falling debris. We remained motionless for what seemed like an age, only moving when I was sure it was safe.

Tara was shaking and her eyes glistened with moisture.

I stood up, pulling her to her feet. The kitchen was virtually destroyed; the living-room was a mess. Only the *Scrabble* board remained unaffected.

'Come on, Steve, let's go,' Tara said, pulling at my arm. Before we could move, there was a tap at the window. An old man's face was pressed against the rain-drizzled glass.

Tara jumped back. 'Who is it, Steve?'

'I don't know,' I said, striding to the door and opening it.

The old man smiled and nodded. 'You okay? I was walking past when it 'appened. I've called the emergency services, they'll be 'ere shortly,' he said with a soft West Country burr.

'We're fine, thanks,' I said. 'And you are …?'

'Jed Pyke, gard'ner and 'andyman. I looks after this place.' He peered in through the open doorway. 'Oh dear, what a mess.' He pushed his way past us.

He went towards the kitchen and then stopped as he reached the *Scrabble* board.

'Well, well. I ain't seen this in years. Use' to belong to Ole Mullen,' he said, grabbing a handful of tiles from Tara's tray.

'Who's Old Mullen?' I asked.

'The previous owner of the cottage, died a few years back now. Made that board hisself, the ole fella.'

'Did he really?'

The old man scratched his weather-worn face with his bony, calloused hand. 'Oh, yeah. He was sorta … obsessed with the game, ya might say. Even named the cottage after it.'

'This cottage? But isn't it called Belsbarc?'

The old man let out a rusty guffaw. 'It's an anagram of the word *scrabble*, me ole son. Clever ain't it!'

Tara put her hand on my shoulder. 'I don't feel well, Steve.'

'Why don't you sit outside on the bench, miss? Fresh air'll do ya good.'

'That's a good idea,' I said.

Tara nodded in agreement.

Outside it was sunny again, and once I knew that Tara was okay, I went back inside.

The old man was now stooped over the *Scrabble* board. I could hear the click of the letters as he placed them on it.

'What are you doing?' I asked somewhat nervously.

'I use' to be good at this game,' he said, placing another tile. 'Look at this for a word.' Just as the old man leaned forward and placed the final letter, the door slammed shut. The wind howled, rattling the windows in their frames. After a few seconds Tara opened the door, looking petrified. Behind her the sky had turned to a swirling mass of blacks and greys. The branches from the tree outside the window scraped the glass; shrubs, and even the longer tufts of grass, swayed ferociously in the roaring wind, and lightning streaked across the sky.

I moved over to the board and stared in horror. Using the word *cane*, which Tara had played earlier, the old man had added five letters to make, *hurricane*.

The Kxrze – Rod Griffiths

The how and why of the curse we may never know. Was it intended to change the world, to have a massive impact on folklore and on so much literature? No one knows.

The first indication that something astonishing had happened was when I met Barney, a vampire named Barney. He had come to seek my advice as a counsellor, needing to talk about whatever was making him miserable.

I tried to keep things as normal as possible.

'What is the problem and what can I do for you?' I always started that way. In medical school we were taught to say 'what seems to be the problem', but I got over that when some kid said, 'I seem to be ill and I thought I'd see you in case I ended up seeming to be dead'.

Barney's problem was quite simple: he was having great difficulty in coming to terms with being a vampire called Barney. He had confided in his friends Nevin and Sharon, and they were no help.

They were driving around in a Ford Fiesta with Nevin and Sharon written on a green plastic thing across the windscreen and beginning to worry about what was happening to them. When he added that the car was a nondescript beige colour, I realised that something enormous was happening. I should have been more diplomatic, but somehow in a moment of indiscretion I said:

'You know, I've never met a vampire called Barney before.'

'Nor have I. No one has and believe me, I've asked a few.'

'Have you asked your family about it?'

A deep frown spread across his face and for a moment I thought I might see a vampire cry.

'I wish I could,' he said eventually. 'They're dead, I can't talk to them.'

Vampires don't die, I thought, well, unless there's been some dirty work with a wooden stake. Having both parents killed seemed unlikely.

'How awful for you, you must have been completely unprepared.'

'Completely.'

I waited for him to go on, but nothing else came.

'How did it happen?'

'They just dropped dead; one moment they were alive, the next they were gone.'

'No wooden stakes, no fire.'

'Nothing,' he said. 'Nothing, they just dropped like an ordinary mortal, and at the same time the weirdest thing happened.'

'Go on.'

'When it happened, they were in the company of ordinary mortals, I mean, my folks were quite well integrated, they did the rounds you know. Helps to prevent misunderstandings my dad always said. OK so picture it, there's three mortals in the room with Mum and Dad and suddenly they both collapse, so what do the mortals do?'

'Mouth to mouth resuscitation would be my guess. Might be tricky with a vampire.'

'Exactly, they're on the floor and folk are jumping on their chests, pounding away for several minutes. It felt like longer, but you get the picture. OK then what does the first aid book say?'

'You tell me.'

'One of the women gets the idea that they need to check to see if they're breathing at all, so she gets a mirror out of her handbag, a little make up mirror. You know the drill, hold it by the mouth and nose and see if it steams up.'

I knew what was coming, you can't see a vampire in a mirror, someone was bound to notice. I sought Barney's eye and for the first time I could see the hint of a smile.

'I guess you thought they'd notice there was no reflection? Yeah?'

'It crossed my mind.'

'Yeah, well it was me that got the shock. I was looking down on the whole thing and I could see my mother's face in the mirror. They weren't just dead, they weren't even vampires any more.'

For a while neither of us could think of anything to say.

Eventually it dawned on me that we were a long way from Nevin and Sharon. 'I should stop interrupting you. There must be more to the story, you haven't told me about Nevin and Sharon.'

'Yeah, well there's not much more to it really, the same thing happened to their parents, in fact almost all the vampires I know have been wiped out. The weird thing is, it's every one with a Z or an X or a K in their name. Some kind of curse that works on spelling.'

'Weird.'

'Yeah, weird alright, but it kills off so many vampires. Worse than that, all record of them disappears and it goes beyond vampires.'

'How do you mean?'

'It's all across science fiction too. Every character with an X or a Z or a K. It's wrecked the genre; I mean can you imagine the Hitch Hiker without the prophet Zarquon, the whole world has changed.'

'You were lucky your parents called you Barney.'

'I didn't used to think so. I got mocked no end.'

'Maybe they were trying to help you blend in.'

'No, it was that TV character Barney the Dinosaur. I was a bit chubby and a kind of purple colour when I was born, and then I puked a sort of green sick down my front. My mum thought I looked like Barney.'

'And it's saved your life.'

'Yeah I guess. Nevin was lucky too, his mum never could spell.'

'She was going to call him Kevin?'

'All part of the blending in agenda, there were a lot of Kevins back then. The arranged marriage with Sharon was all part of the deal.'

'Is there anyone you could talk to? It's OK to come here but I charge by the hour.'

'You mean like a girlfriend?'

'Perhaps called Barbie?'

'I'm there already, she's called Annabell, another cute blond with a doll named after her.' He sighed. 'There are no cool people left.'

'How does she spell her name?'

'The usual way I guess.'

I had his attention, there must have been something in my voice.

'There's two ways,' I said. 'Does she have an 'e' on the end?'

'Why does it matter?'

'Annabell without the 'e' is a cute doll for two-year-olds, Annabelle with an 'e' is the horror doll from the Conjuring movie, which I might remind you is based on a true story.'

'She has an 'e',' he said. 'I'm sure of it. Hey, I feel better already.'

The Last Siberian Tigress – Tony Judge

The cherry tree is blooming in the street outside. The bones in her neck creak as she cranes towards the window from her armchair, trying to catch a glimpse of the ethereal pink. On her right side is the small gas fire, on her left the low table, where she keeps the samovar. Sometimes she forgets to put the samovar on, so she drinks yesterday's cold tea with her breakfast jam and bread. The fire is a rare luxury, reserved for special occasions, such as visits from grandson Misha.

He doesn't visit so often now. Not since he moved to Leningrad. She still calls it Leningrad, cannot bring herself to utter the hated old-new name, St Petersburg. Misha had to leave. It's such a good job he has there, something to do with computers. He's explained it to her, but the words are just words. She has nothing to hang them on. If he said he was a doctor, or a farmer, or a train driver, or a soldier, she could understand that. She knows all about soldiers; she married a soldier, was a soldier herself once.

When the call came from Comrade Stalin, as a good communist, she had known her duty. There was no need for anyone to dragoon her. She presented herself at the local party headquarters on the shores of Lake Baikal, begging, no, demanding to join the army. The training was over in a few weeks and before she'd had a chance to say goodbye to her parents, she was hauling her kit bag onto the station platform with all the others from her unit. Two weeks she spent on that lice-infested troop train, fending off the advances of her male comrades, watching the unknowable vastness of the motherland unfolding on the other side of the window.

Those were different times, heroism was in the air. She wonders often if certain generations are inherently more heroic than others, or if it is just the demands of history that make them so. It is one of those unanswerable questions, like, 'Why do men love to drink so?' You can sit and turn your brain upside down and inside out and never come up with an answer that will stand up in a gentle breeze. So why waste your time pondering these mysteries?

There is a photograph on her mantelpiece. A young man, in Red Army uniform circa 1943, is sitting at a table, holding up a glass of vodka and winking at the camera. He looks tanned and strong, ready to take on the world. It is this memory of Sergei that she prefers; the more recent photos are packed away in a trunk. They never see daylight anymore.

She looks across at the cheap, plastic-topped dining table, all they could afford on their pensions. If she squints, it's still possible to imagine him sitting there, watching TV with his vodka in front of him, polluting the flat with his roll-ups. It was always vodka and cigarettes with Sergei. She would put a plate in front of him with some slices of sausage, pickles and good rye bread on it. When she returned from the market, the bread was usually untouched and the meat and pickle barely so. Pleading with him was useless. 'Sergei, eat the bread, if you eat nothing else, please, eat the bread!' She had learned this on operations, out in the woods, fighting the fascists. The others would waste space carrying sweets and vodka, when they could get them. She would take as much bread as she could stuff into her pack. It always pulled you through. But Sergei would just smile and pour himself more vodka and then raise his glass to her, the way they did in the army. It infuriated her and he knew it. He did not want the bread in his stomach. It would act as a sponge and slow down the hit from the drink. That was the last thing he wanted.

Misha doesn't drink spirits, only a little beer or wine. Misha has sense; he wants to keep his wits sharp for his job. You need to be crystal clear when it comes to computers, that's what he tells her.

A young man came calling yesterday, the third time this week. He claims to have a special deal on the insurance for her flat. This time he pushed some documents under her nose. 'Sign, Baba … sign! It's for your own benefit.' She had refused and he had become agitated, a little threatening. She wished that Misha was with her, to deal with him. She had just written a note for her neighbour, the one who helped with the shopping. It was just her usual list with her little flourish of a signature at the bottom. Before he left, the man had taken a small object from his pocket. It was sleek, pleasing to look at, like the silver make up compact that she keeps in her jewellery box. He pointed it at the note on the table and pressed a button. When the flash went off, she realised that he was taking a picture. She protested, but he was already sweeping up his documents and striding towards the door.

She wishes again that Misha would come, but then thinks better of it. There is something in the man's expression that reminds her of Dmitry Karpov, her old unit commander; a deadness in the eyes that makes you wonder what might happen if you cross him, if he knows any limits. With Karpov, there had been no limits. The fascist prisoners in their care had discovered that on more than one occasion. She had been sickened at first, revolted at seeing the defenceless killed like that, but she had told herself, 'The motherland needs men like Karpov. We should celebrate him as a hero.' She had learned then to keep such 'hard secrets', as she called them. Hard secrets were the kind that meant the difference between someone living and dying, and that someone was usually you.

These are different times, she thinks. Something has perverted the heroic, patriotic impulses of our grandchildren and turned so many of them into gangsters. Her fear of the young man is tinged with pity. He will never have the opportunity to know true heroism and the comradeship of sacrifice.

When she met Sergei, they were both on active service, fighting with the partisans along the shifting front line west of Moscow. She was carrying a long-barrelled sniper's rifle. It was heavy, but she managed. He had laughed at her, 'How can you shoot that thing? You can hardly carry it!' She had bridled with anger, but kept quiet. When he saw that she could shoot a Fritz in the head from a kilometre away, he soon learned to respect her. At first, the recoil from the rifle bruised her shoulder badly, but she had stuffed kapok into her tunic to absorb the impact. This is the shoulder that aches now, from morning to night. It is arthritis, the same arthritis that has ruined her hips and knees, keeping her in bed most days until mid-morning.

It was not long after they met that she had slept with Sergei for the first time. You had to take love when it was available then, you might be dead tomorrow. She had wrapped her legs around him and clawed his back raw. 'My little Siberian Tigress,' he had called her. The nickname had stuck, even with the other members of the unit, although they thought it referred solely to her fighting spirit. Sergei would grin like a wolf and wink at her, whenever he heard one of them using it.

She thinks, if she could just lose twenty years she would be able to stand up to the man who came calling. She knows that she will never tell Misha about him. Misha does not have that Karpov look. He is one of the gentle ones. If she tells him, he might try to do something heroic and end up getting himself shot in some alley. It will have to be another of her hard secrets.

There is a wind blowing along the street now. The blossom is streaming past her window, reminding her of when, as a small girl, she would eat cherries straight from the trees in Uncle Max's garden. It was high above the shore, with a view over the profound blue depths of Baikal.

After the war, they settled in Moscow, Sergei's home town. She missed the country, so they found a plot at the end of a bus route and built a tiny dacha. In the years of their strength, it yielded so many crops of potatoes, cabbages, beans and onions. And fruit! Oh the strawberries and the plums! They gave it up when Sergei couldn't work the ground anymore. She no longer craves the lake shore of her childhood. She remembers the bitter winters, even worse than Moscow's. She has not been to their little dacha in the woods for years, but still dreams of plunging her fingers one final time into the deep black earth and pulling up a handful of sweet new potatoes.

Someone is banging on the door, loud, impatient knocks.

'Misha? Is that you … Misha?'

But she knows that Misha is not coming.

The Million-year-old Man In My Head – Rod Griffiths

Since the 1990s, a class of drugs called atypical antipsychotics have been used to treat schizophrenia. How did a class of drugs come to be called atypical; where did they come from?

There is a million-year-old man in my head. You might think I'm crazy, but I call him Alfred. I'm sure that is not his name, but it is an old name. There was a king of England a thousand years ago whose name was Alfred. It is not popular in these modern times. Alfie has just made it into the top-ten list of boy's names, behind Oliver, Jack and Harry. I don't like Alfie; it sounds much too familiar for a man who is a million years old. I am careful to call him Alfred; respect is important.

I may be wrong about the million years, it's a rough guess. Maybe he's only seven hundred thousand years old, but a million sounds better and it might even be longer. Counting like we do is not one of Alfred's strengths. He is far older than anything I know, apart from rocks, or the moon.

Alfred lives in my head, and most of the time I don't know that he's there. He thinks very slowly, so slowly that I don't notice the bit of my brain that he's borrowed. The only hints I have – that give me a clue he is there – are his memories, memories that cannot possibly be mine.

Of course, I hear you say, we all have false memories. Déjà Vu, the neurologists call it. I've looked it up; it's really just a trick of the brain, not really a false memory at all. It is something that happens when two parts of the brain get a bit out of step with each other. It always works the same way: something happens and you think it has happened before. It may be a room you walk into, or something someone says, but there is always something in the present that feels like a repeat. Some scientists think that the problem lies in the temporal lobe; that's the part of the brain that you would hit if you drilled a hole somewhere between your ear and your eyebrow; not recommended at all, and it probably wouldn't cure Déjà Vu. Others think the problem could be in the Hippocampus: another part of the brain, near the temporal lobe, not a place for hippos to camp, they'd never fit in. People who suffer from epilepsy centred on the temporal lobe have Déjà Vu more often than average, though over sixty percent of the population get it at some time or another.

What I have is not Déjà Vu. Alfred's memories are nothing like that. I remember passing planets in space, looking out of the porthole and seeing planets that do not resemble any of those that NASA has been good enough to photograph for us. I remember planets with two suns, bright stars in patterns and constellations that no one has ever recorded, at least not on earth. If I were having Déjà Vu, then I'd be in a spaceship, passing a planet, and thinking I'd been there before. Sitting in an armchair remembering planets with two suns is not the same thing. I'm being a bit pedantic here, going on about it too much; it's just that Alfred has seen these planets because he was a spaceman once. Well, not spaceman, sort of space living entity of some kind.

He has been on Earth for a long time. His spaceship crashed and all that's left of Alfred is a form of parasite in my brain. That may be the wrong word: symbiosis, is what the relationship should be called, except it's so much harder to spell. Parasites cause trouble, but Alfred doesn't do me any harm, unless I tell someone about him. If I do that then some people call me mad.

I'm not schizophrenic. I'm not hearing voices. Alfred doesn't speak; I just know he's there because I share some of his memories. That's not really any different from reading stuff in books; that's just sharing other people's memories, except that those ones are written down before they get in your head, but once they are in your head, what's the difference? If you see a movie and you remember it very clearly, as if you were there, as if it was real, is that a hallucination?

Alfred is not the only one of his kind. There were many other space entities with him when he came. He can keep in touch with them, by some sort of telepathy. Some of them are very clever; they know loads of things like chemistry and stuff like that. Years ago when they arrived, I think they were similar to proper people with arms and legs or physical tendrils or something so that they could work their spaceship. They came from a different dimension, and Alfred says they were invisible. I've struggled a bit to understand that, it's all to do with quantum physics and stuff. I read somewhere that all the molecules in the world are mostly empty space. Protons and neutrons in the middle, and electrons whizzing around, but mostly empty space. I'm not studying physics and, from what I can tell, all that quantum stuff takes a lot to mug up, but I think what Alfred tells me is that they lived in all that space between the electrons and protons.

Now, after all these years Alfred's people are reduced to living in borrowed brains like mine. If I concentrate very hard, I can communicate with Alfred, but it's not easy. Although he's very clever, his brain works extremely slowly; I think it's to do with him being so old, or living such a long time, or maybe that's quantum too. Anyway, it takes me ages to find out anything from him.

You would think I could learn a lot from Alfred, like I wouldn't need history lessons, but it doesn't seem to work like that. I can't get him to pay attention to those details. I guess if you are a million years old then 1066, or Henry the Eighth are just like a second or two, like a fly whizzing past. Alfred only remembers big stuff, like the ice age. I tried to ask him about dinosaurs, which was dumb of me because it turns out they lived over two hundred million years ago and even Alfred isn't that old.

I did wonder how he could be a million years old and me be only just past twenty. Apparently his kind have learned to sort of jump from one brain to another. It takes a huge amount of energy to be able to do that, so he has to save up his strength for ages, and after a jump he is completely worn out and can't do anything for years. He got to me from my grandma and he made the jump when I was three months old. He didn't really get his strength back until I was eighteen, so I only noticed him when I left school.

When I first heard him, I told a few friends about him. I thought they'd be excited; I mean it's not everyone who has a million-year-old space entity in their head.

I should have thought about it more because the next thing I knew I was sent to see a doctor. I didn't tell her the whole story, but I had to tell her some of it because some of my mates had ratted on me. She said it must be stress from going to university. She said she'd see me in a month, so after that I kept quiet about Alfred. Like I said, I'm not schizophrenic. I don't have a split mind, there's just me, and Alfred borrowing a bit of my brain.

I kept my head down and concentrated on work. I got into a routine where I would only try to listen to Alfred at certain times of day. I first tried to do it just before I went to sleep; except it was hard to remember what he said when I woke up in the morning. I gave that up and tried going for walks in the country on Sundays. That worked much better and I took a notebook so I could jot things down. I think other folk thought I was a poet or something. I got funny looks if I talked aloud, or if my face gave something away, so I used to put my headphones in my ears all the time. Anyone who looked would think I was listening to pop or the radio or whatever. It gave me a good excuse if I ignored someone I was supposed to know, and mostly people left me alone.

It took most of the next year to work things out properly. Alfred's real problem is the lack of certain micronutrients. These are complex chemicals like vitamins, except the ones he and his people need are not like the ones we need, and they don't exist on earth. Apparently, it never occurred to Alfred's people that these things might not exist in other places, so they didn't bring enough with them in their spaceship.

Around about the time I worked that out, just before I was due to take my finals, Alfred got very excited because some of his people had managed to get jobs in a pharmaceutical company. What I mean is that the people whose brains they were living in had those jobs. Alfred worked with these other space entities.

This was very difficult for them because their brains work at such different speeds to ours, but Alfred said they were making progress.

They had a major breakthrough because they managed to make some of the right chemical, but it wasn't like any of the drugs that this company had made before. There was a real risk that the stuff might end up on the scrap heap, dismissed as being a research blind alley.

The tricky problem was how to get the stuff from the laboratory into the brains of people who had Alfreds in their brains. Plenty of people my age take all sorts of chemicals, but Alfred says that some of those can really harm his people, so we have to be careful.

I had a dilemma about my exams. Should I just ignore Alfred until the exams were over, or should I try to get Alfred to help? Obviously, he wouldn't be any use in the actual exam because he can't think quickly enough. He did seem to be able to remember a lot of stuff in the bit of my brain he was borrowing, so I wondered if there was some way he could lend it back to me in the exam.

I got through the first few papers, no problem, but in the last one, I got tuned into Alfred too much. I'd already written a lot before I got completely connected to Alfred and then without realising I ended up just sitting there, apparently doing nothing and saying nothing for hours. I was so into Alfred that I didn't even notice when they took me out in a wheelchair. I think it was just because Alfred thinks so slowly. Thinking like him made me seem like I was in a trance. They said I was catatonic at the hospital, but that's just them going on about schizophrenia again. I wasn't catatonic, I was just talking to Alfred. It turned out eventually that I'd written enough to pass the exams, but I still ended up in hospital.

That wasn't so bad, because that's where I had the idea that liberated Alfred. Ah, but was it his idea? You might think that, but Alfred thinks so slowly that it had to be me. If I'd had to wait for him, I might have been in that place for a hundred years.

What I thought was this: what if I could convince the doctors that those chemicals that Alfred's people had invented were good for people like me. If they made it into pills and I took the pills, it would be good for Alfred. That's what I thought. A pharmaceutical company made the stuff, so it could be prescribed like any other medicine. Of course, the stuff isn't like any of the drugs that have been used for mental illness before. No matter, they hadn't found any other use for it, so I concentrated very hard on telling Alfred to tell his people to get the stuff made into pills. It meant hours of concentration. That meant the doctors kept on thinking that I was a serious case of catatonia, but that wasn't a bad thing because it just meant that all the doctors came to think that I was a bad case and that nothing else worked on me. What better case to try a new kind of drug. They ended up calling them atypical antipsychotic drugs.

I could tell straight away that it was making Alfred better. The next step was to make sure that all Alfred's friends could get the drug for the people they were living in. That wasn't so hard because it's easy to fake hearing voices and being catatonic. I could feel Alfred getting stronger, but I knew he'd need a bit more energy to make the jump into being independent and getting his spaceship going.

I didn't want him just leaping across to someone else, like one of the nurses. That wouldn't be fair to them. I needed to know Alfred could get to his spaceship. It couldn't be far away; it must be just sitting there hiding among the molecules. Once I was clear about that, I set about making everyone think I was so depressed that ECT was the only hope. It just needed one good jolt of electricity to energise Alfred and he was gone.

* * *

The doctor asked me how the space ship worked, but what with one thing or another I'd never got around to asking Alfred, and anyway it's all quantum stuff and beyond me.

The other question they kept asking me was what happened to the rest of Alfred's people. As far as I know they left the same way as Alfred, once their hosts had taken the tablets.

I don't think the doctors believed my story because not all the people who take the tablets are cured like me. That's what the doctors said. I don't know why they think that's an important question. It seems perfectly obvious to me that everyone with hallucinations doesn't have an Alfred: some of them have schizophrenia, and they need help.

The Old Dog – Mike Alma

In a small, Kentish fishing village everyone knew everyone, except no one knew 'Flic' Fletcher – no one wanted to. His Christian name was unknown, as were the origins of his nickname … not that anyone bothered to find out. Behind his back he was 'that miserable old bugger, Fletcher'.

At ninety-eight he had outlived those contemporaries who might have known him in his younger days. He spoke to no one on his brief excursions to the shops, and anyone getting in his way received a bountiful broadside of invective. He never smiled.

No one had ever seen the inside of his cottage and few had ventured past his front gate. It was rumoured that, years before, someone had been met by the twin barrels of a shotgun, a greeting that had been frowned upon by the local 'Bobby'. Sensibly, armed support had been obtained from county headquarters, but the old man had met them at his front gate, without fuss, to hand over the inoperable, rusted weapon to the amused officers.

More recently, the vicar, determined to reach out to a lost sheep, took half-a-dozen steps beyond the front gate, before spotting twin barrels protruding from behind the front door. His retreat was less than graceful and it required the protracted presence of smelling salts and several generous measures of brandy before he was sufficiently revived to contemplate a visit to the police station, a couple of miles away, to report the threat against his holy skin.

Unbeknownst to him, the incident had been reported to a patrolling constable who had, immediately, gone to the old man's cottage, to find that the 'shotgun' was no more than two black-painted broom handles taped together. He saw no reason to confiscate two broom-handles, though he did insist on removing the notice, nailed to the gate, threatening to shoot any trespassers.

The vicar, on turning up at the police station, determined to press charges against the old man, was promptly breathalysed and found to be over the limit. His subsequent appearance in front of the magistrate didn't help much, since the 'beak' didn't like the fellow (hated his sanctimonious sermons) and had great pleasure in banning him from driving for a year. The vicar, incapable of covering his parish on a push-bike, resigned soon after.

'Flic' Fletcher went about life without change. He had no relatives, no visitors and his only mail (left in a box by the front gate) was bills from 'the electric'. He had no telephone and no television. Beyond that, there's nothing more you could say about him ... apart from the undeniable fact that he was a miserable old bugger.

Every time he left his cottage, he turned his back on the sea, no more than a five-minute walk away, down past the harbour. He would go to the shops for his provisions, or he would be at home, curtains drawn, doing nothing more than fuelling people's imaginations.

Until, one day, he didn't turn his back on the sea. That white-haired, wizened old man shut his garden gate, pausing to ensure it wouldn't be blown open by a mischievous gust of wind, and headed towards the harbour, with the green seas beyond. Folk stopped to watch his shuffling progress across centuries-worn cobbles, aware that something exceptional was taking place. By the time he reached the harbour wall there were thirty or more people closely watching his laborious trek across the giant stones – every step, somehow, was redemption ... every faltering movement erasing those years of distrust, dislike and open animosity towards him. He reached the end of the harbour wall where it curved awkwardly to challenge the driving breakers from the north, pausing with both hands resting on a bollard, steadying himself against the wind that threatened to pluck him, like a leaf, from his place. With one hand, he reached out towards the wind, stretching for an unseen place beyond the waves – beyond the horizon. The watchers, barely daring to breathe, saw him slowly crumple. He closed his eyes on the world and, without pain, was gone.

They carried him home, letting themselves in with the key he had left in the lock, unable to believe how sensitive his face had become, a gentle smile softening his gaunt features, as if he had just greeted someone special. In fact, there was a lot that people found hard to believe, both then, when they saw how spotless and warm the cottage was, and later, after the solicitor had been through all the papers, discovering the truth about Richard Fletcher.

Seventy years earlier, while he and his tiny boat were darting in and out – in and out – plucking frightened young men from the beaches of Dunkirk – flicking the rudder one way, then the other, dodging bombs, boats and bodies – his wife and two sweet babies were lying crushed beneath a demolished air-raid shelter … 'you'll be safe in there, love …' He had never shed the guilt that had consumed his smile and his laughter – that had hardened his heart and stolen all hope, leaving him nothing.

He would have swapped the many men whose lives he had saved, for the three broken bodies he had returned to – the very reasons for his existence. The letters from those saved soldiers were testimony to his bravery, but most had never been opened, until the solicitor sliced the past into the present, by cutting into the secrets hidden inside the envelopes.

The cottage was a soft place – a beautiful home, waiting for a family that would never return. The beds were made and the wardrobes and drawers were full – a place frozen in time. Photographs round the cottage pictured gentle, lovely people, from a permanent yesterday.

It was the funeral director who, absent-mindedly, picked up a picture of the dead man's wife, studied it for a while, appreciating her soft, monochrome beauty, before replacing it on the mantelshelf …

'The old dog!'

The Price – Damon Lord

'You two: go. You know what to do.' I gestured to the two soldiers and they slunk off towards the cottage. My orders were to negotiate first. They were back up. I entered the blacksmith's workshop.

'I have a commission for you, from the King himself,' I said, striding forward.

The blacksmith did not turn around. He was hammering away, leaning over his anvil, working a piece of metal into a rough curve. 'I don't do that sort of work any more,' he said. He continued working.

'Why?'

'It costs too much,' he mumbled.

'We have gold. Money.'

'I have no interest in that.'

'Land.'

'No.'

'Women,' I said. 'I know your wife is dead. Delicious slave girls from the northern edges of the Empire breasts the size of august ragberries, sweet as honey.' That would easily buy the services of most men.

He continued to ignore me.

'Boys?' I asked. What was his price?

He flung the horseshoe into a barrel of water, and turned to me. At last, I could see his full frame. He was broad shouldered, filled with muscles and blanketed in sweat. He towered over me, casting me in shadow from the forge fire.

'No. It costs too much.' He spoke with thunder. He weighted his hammer in his hand. 'I'm a family man. I don't work like that. Now go.'

'Name your price.' This was going to be difficult. I was under orders from the King himself. If I didn't come back with the goods, my life would be forfeit.

'I cannot be bought.' He raised his hammer up and brought it down into the palm of his hand. He didn't even flinch.

I blinked. There was one more thing to try, before it became drastic. 'Look, let me reason with you. You know what the King is like. He's sent me here to bring back a sword imbued with an invulnerability charm. You're renowned for it, and if you don't make it, my family's life will be in jeopardy.'

Outside, I heard a low whistle. The soldiers were ready. The blacksmith raised himself up to tower above me. He flung his hammer across the workshop. I heard something break. 'What do I care? What of my family? It costs them too much!'

'How much are your family worth to you?' I said.

'More than anything. I'd do anything for them. But not that.'

'I was hoping you'd say that,' I said. Now it was my turn. I whistled long and hard, and the two soldiers stormed in, pulling the blacksmith's daughter after them. They held her hard; she struggled but was weak against the soldiers.

'Nu'er,' the blacksmith sobbed. That must be her name, I thought.

'We have a deal then,' I said. I had broken him and my family was safe. 'Your daughter's life in return for a sword. And to show I'll keep my side of the bargain, I'll still reward you with gold.'

'You don't know what you ask of me.'

'A sword. A charm. It can't be that difficult?'

He looked again with mournful longing at his daughter and then strode over to the window. 'Look,' he said, and beckoned me over. Outside, in the distance, was a small graveyard. 'My other children. You have the last of my family, my beloved Nu'er.'

'Plague?' I asked.

'No,' he said. 'I killed them making my previous charmed swords. That's why I don't make them anymore.'

'You mean—'

'For the making to work, it requires the magical harming of an innocent, someone beloved. Beloved to me. She's all I've got left.'

I looked down at the ground and then back at the child. She was small and wide-eyed, a tear forming in her left eye. For a moment I saw my own beloved daughter there. I could not let it happen to my family.

I let out a deep breath. 'Can it be done without killing her? Will she survive?'

The blacksmith sighed. 'Yes.'

'Then do it.' I made to step away from the child, but the blacksmith grabbed me by the shoulder. Before anyone could react he shoved me towards my soldiers and the girl.

'No you don't. You will hold my daughter, look her in the eyes, so she will remember your face and know it when she comes to judge you.'

At the anvil he raised his hammer to deliver the first blow to the steel. The child's skin began to glow. As he struck, the first blood welled out and the girl screamed.

The Prineville Trail – Polly Robinson

She could feel Trig was flagging. He snickered avoiding tumuli and moat-like cracks in the parched rocky ground of the Oregon Badlands. He reared as a snake shot across the trail. Netta fell back, grappled for the reins, the stirrups, missed, landed hard. She lay motionless, winded, watching the rattler, listening to its tail, conscious of the scent of wild thyme in the air.

The rattle stopped and the snake slipped away into the bluebunch wheatgrass. Netta lay still until her breathing steadied, then raised herself onto an elbow testing her limbs. Felt her ribs. Seemed she was intact. She whistled and Trig returned snorting, tossing his head. If he were a person, he'd look sorry. She reached for the canteen, sipped; she had to eke it out. Netta cupped water in her hand; he supped it.

The wild thyme wafted to her again. She thought of Granny Mo, showing her how to rinse thyme and put it into soup at exactly the right moment.

'It strengthens a pale pot of soup, Netta,' Granny Mo said, 'brings happiness to the tongue.' Me oh my, that was a helluva long time ago.

Another half-day's trail before she'd get to Prineville to the north. An endless vista of rugged paths and ponderosa pines stretched ahead. The gin-like scent from the ancient western juniper woodlands away to the left reminded her of Prairie City. Only tumbleweed broke the still of the day. Riding chaps and sweat chafed her legs. She wanted to rest her eyes but had to keep alert. The Paiute shouldn't be this far southeast and raids were s'posed to have ceased according to the hands at Prairie City. Her thoughts went back there. Prairie City, where wild horses drank from the springs at the edge of the desert. Prairie City, where a drunken bum had tried to feel her up.

She heard him come up behind her, crooning.

'Netta. Oh, Netta.' He must've heard the barkeep call her by name.

She'd stubbed out her cheroot and shouldered past him out through the saloon doors, waited a couple of seconds to see if he'd follow. He did. She stalked into the darkness of the alley between the saloon and the grain store.

'Netta. Oh, Netta.'

Netta took no notice of him, kept walking, a knot of tension in her stomach. She could hear him fumbling with his holster. She glanced behind; there was enough light from the saloon window to see him hooking the guns and holster over his shoulder. Then she heard him undo his belt; it clinked against the holster. She knew both were now carried around his neck.

She slid into a doorway and waited. Heard him cuss, 'Dammit, baby, where you gone? You waiting on ole Snake Eyes, ole Jake? Huh? Teasing me, Eh?' He cussed again as he tripped, righted himself. 'Netta. Oh, Netta. You know you wannit. Come to daddy, baby.'

She almost laughed aloud as moonlight briefly showed him holding his pants up with one hand and feeling his way along the clapboard with the other. It was enough for her to choose her moment. She could hear and smell his fluting fetid gin-breath as he almost lurched into her. She gripped the belt, kicked his shin, shifted and swung behind him hauling the belt tight. The belt wound around one of the guns, the other chucked up the alley; she twisted the belt tighter. He arched, bucked and pulled her arms, unwittingly tightening the belt around his neck as he tried to get her off him. She held on knowing what would happen if she eased up for a second. He bucked again, this time his heel connected with her leg and she went down. In an instant, she was back up again renewing the twisting tension on the belt. Another half twist, and another. Spit frothed from his mouth. His final breaths rattled. She held on. It seemed like hours before he went limp. She lowered him to the ground.

Netta said, 'No one treats Granny Mo's girl like that.' She whistled. Trig joined her at the bottom of the alley.

Her knuckles shone white on the saddle horn as she journeyed on towards Prineville across the Prineville Trail.

The Rhubarb Triangle – Tim Butler

The crow flew high and free. Wheeling and gliding on midsummer thermals, it passed over the tiny villages, remote farms and endless bleak moorland of the North York Moors. Spiralling over a stony village square, it let out a loud 'caw' of joy, followed by several more caws of annoyance. It had forgotten about the item it had been carrying in its beak and was now watching it fall rapidly to earth.

In the same spot, several feet closer to the ground and less than half an hour later, PC Terri Arswhistle was making use of the outside seating at Edith's Tea Rooms to interview Maureen and Arthur Tiddeswell.

'So, Mrs Tiddeswell, it was you that noticed the bird flying over?'

'Yes that's right, love. It was a crow wasn't it, Arthur?'

'Aye,' said Arthur.

'And you saw it drop something as it passed over?'

'Yes, love, it went right down into Arthur's cup, didn't it, Arthur?'

'Aye,' said Arthur.

'And I said to Arthur "a bird's done its business in your tea", didn't I, Arthur?'

'Aye,' said Arthur.

'But then it floated to the top and it wasn't bird muck at all,' said Maureen. 'It was an eye.'

'An eye?' said Terri.

'Aye,' said Arthur.

'Well we didn't know what to do with it, so we told Edith.'

'The lady who runs the teashop?' said Terri.

'That's right, love,' Maureen continued. 'And she said that it was a matter for the police, so she called Sergeant Rowbotham and he sent you.'

'And where is the cup now?'

'It's under there,' said Maureen, pointing to a table with a white tablecloth draped over it. 'Edith put a cloth over it.'

The substantial figure of Edith Ploughman appeared at Terri's elbow. 'To keep out prying eyes and nosey parkers,' she said. 'I left everything as it was – I expect you'll be wanting to cordon it off with some of that yellow tape, get those forensical people up from Scarborough.'

'Let's take it one step at a time shall we?' said Terri. 'Can I take a look at the scene of the incident?'

'Right you are, love,' said Edith, and she pulled back the cloth to reveal a cup and saucer sitting in a pool of spilt tea. Terri peered into the cup; a large dark eye peered back at her.

'Who do you think it belonged to?' asked Edith.

'Well from the size of it I'd say either Daisy or Buttercup.'

'Oh my God,' said Edith. 'A woman! Well she had beautiful brown eyes whoever she was, poor thing.'

'She was a cow,' said Terri.

Edith looked aghast. 'Well I don't know how you do things down in Leeds,' she began, 'but up here we don't speak ill of the dead.'

'No, Mrs Ploughman, the eye belongs to an actual cow, or possibly a horse. Look at the size of it. It's as big as a snooker ball.'

'Oh,' said Edith. 'So how did it come to land in one of my teacups?'

'That's what I'm here to find out,' said Terri.

'It's a portent,' said a woman with a high wavering voice. 'A black crow and a bloody eye. Some evil is abroad.'

'Don't mind Morag,' said Edith. 'She's one of those mediocre people.'

'I think you mean medium,' said Morag.

'Do I?' said Edith.

Terri sensed that a situation might be brewing and stepped in. 'PC Terri Arswhistle. Pleased to meet you.'

'Morag McKinley,' said Morag, her bangles jangling tunefully as she shook Terri's hand. 'If you need any help with your investigation just let me know. I've been able to assist the police in cases before. I have the gift you see.' She turned Terri's hand over and began to examine her palm. Terri snatched it back quickly, before she could make any pronouncements. Being told you were going to meet a tall dark stranger wasn't always what you needed to hear in this job.

'I'll bear that in mind, Ms McKinley,' said Terri.

'You do that,' said Morag. 'It's a full moon tonight; you'd best be careful if you're out on the moors.'

'Why?' said Terri. 'What's out there, werewolves?'

'Just be careful,' said Morag, and she swept off in a cloud of gauzy scarves and patchouli oil.

Back at the station Terri ran through what had happened at Edith's with Sergeant Rowbotham, but she suspected that he'd already been apprised of the situation before she arrived. He certainly seemed bursting to tell her something.

'So it was just a cow's eye then, Arswhistle?'

'Yes, Sarge.'

'And this passing crow managed to drop it right in a teacup.'

'That's what they said, Sarge.'

'Bloody good shot that eh, Arswhistle?'

'Yes, Sarge.' Terri could sense that he was building up to something.

'In fact, I'd call it a bullseye!' The sergeant exploded into booming laughter. His eyes streamed and his face turned red as he fought to regain his composure. Terri smiled politely. Sergeant Rowbotham was a good copper, she told herself; she could learn a lot of things from him. But comedy was probably not one of them.

'Anything else come in while I've been out, Sarge?'

'Nothing as big as Edith's IT problem.'

'Sarge?'

'I.T.' he said. 'Eye-tea!'

He was off again. Terri wondered if one day he might actually pass out from lack of oxygen while laughing at one of his own jokes; she was sure it was possible. Finally, he wiped the tears away and brought himself under control.

'There's this.' He handed her a pink slip of paper noting the details of a call from the public. 'Some walker up by Rounton's Farm complaining about a smell.'

'A smell, Sarge, on a farm?'

'I know, I know. It's probably some southerner who wants all the sheep shit clearing up before he walks over a field. Just have a look for me, Arswhistle. I told him we'd look into it.'

'Right, Sarge. Will do.'

Terri headed back to the car.

Rounton Farm was miles away from anywhere, remote even by North York Moors standards. Luckily, the walker had given a pretty good description of where the smell was occurring. It was probably silage or muck spreading, but they were right to check it out. If people didn't think you'd act on their calls, then they'd stop making them. Although, thought Terri, it would probably have the same effect if we just told people that we'd acted on their information. Then she dismissed this thought as being unworthy of a police officer. This was a worthwhile shout. Sergeant Rowbotham may be a bit old school, but he was a proper copper through and through. He wouldn't just send her out on a fool's errand, would he?

There was a right of way which cut through the top end of Rounton Farm. Its isolation attracted only the most dedicated walkers. Terri parked up where what passed for the road gave out into a rutted track and set off on foot. According to the map, the path went up the edge of the field and towards a copse on the brow of the hill. Terri headed for the trees. She sniffed the air; there was a bit of a whiff about the place and it was getting stronger as she climbed the hill. It didn't smell like fertilizer or even manure; it was a rotten smell. Something had gone bad around here. She took a tissue from her pocket and clamped it over her mouth and nose. Southerner or not, she wasn't surprised the walker had called it in.

She hadn't seen any likely cause on the way up, so the source of the smell had to be in the copse. Up close it was thicker than it had seemed from the bottom of the hill. The trees grew into one another and blocked out the light. The smell was also thicker. It was starting to make her retch. Maybe she should go back to the station and get some proper gear from SOCO? And how would it look when she returned in a full space suit and respirator to find two dozen eggs dumped under a tree? Terri decided to press on. She pulled back a branch to look into the wood and immediately jumped back as a group of startled crows burst through the trees and into the air. A murder of crows, she thought; what would Morag McKinley make of that?

Terri soon saw what the crows had been interested in. In a clearing lay the remains of a large Friesian cow. The carcass had been torn into several pieces and the undergrowth was stained darkly with blood. She found the head a few feet away and quickly ascertained that it was indeed missing an eye. Well that's one case closed, she thought, before she hurried back out of the trees to throw up.

One bottle of water and half a pack of Polos later, Terri was calling on Farmer Rounton at home. The farmhouse was in a bad way. The roof sagged in the middle and large chunks of plaster were missing from the walls. One of the upstairs windows was broken and had been repaired by taping an empty fertilizer bag to the frame. By the front gate was a mouldy looking wooden box with a handwritten cardboard sign advertising 'Fresh egges. 60 pens duzzen'. The letter 'r' in fresh was written back to front.

Terri went to knock at the front door but noticed noises coming from round the back. She called out,

'Mr Rounton, it's the police. Can I have a quick word please?' There was no reply but the sounds had stopped. There was now the silence of someone being very, very quiet. It was a sound that Terri knew well; a guilty silence. She wondered if she should have called in before she came down to the farm.

'Come on,' she told herself. 'This isn't Leeds. There isn't a junkie hiding behind the wall waiting to jump on me.'

Around the corner was a large, ragged poly tunnel with the wind blowing through it. Sections of plastic flapped and slapped against the struts. Inside, a large thickset man with his back to her was doing something on a workbench, and he had a pile of rusty tin cans and a bag of white pellets next to him.

'Mr Rounton?' Terri called from the doorway, but the man didn't turn round. Maybe he couldn't hear with all the wind. She moved inside and tried again, a bit louder this time.

'Mr Rounton. Are you aware that there's a dead cow up in the copse near Allerton Lane?'

Suddenly he spun round. He had a long butcher's knife in one hand and a hunk of gristly meat in the other.

'It weren't me!' he shouted. In the confined space of the tunnel he looked huge.

'I just want to ask you a few questions that's all, Mr Rounton. There's nothing to worry about.'

'It weren't me!' he said again, waving the knife in the air for emphasis.

'What the bloody hell's going on here?' There was another man behind her, older from the sound of him. Terri didn't want to turn round to face him and leave her back exposed to the knife.

'I'm PC Terri Arswhistle, sir. There's been an incident in the field near Allerton Lane. I'm here to ask—'

'Incident in a field. My field? Well you'd better tell me about it. Martin, what do you think you're doing in here? Those pigs'll be up to their knees in shit by now. Go get 'em mucked out.'

The huge man stared down at the floor like a naughty schoolboy.

'Yes, Dad,' was all he said, before flinging the knife and the meat down on the bench and rushing past Terri.

'He's a good lad but he needs to be told sometimes. Now what's this about an incident in my field?'

'Would you be Peter Rounton, sir?'

'Course I bloody am and I know who you are, so why don't you tell me what's going on?'

'There's a dead cow, sir. It's been attacked.'

'Probably some tourists letting their dogs off the lead. That or those bastard badgers.'

'Have you seen any dogs or large animals running loose?'

'Large animals? Only our lad.'

'Martin was it? That's your son.'

'Aye. What of it?'

'He was cutting up some meat when I got here. Can you tell me what that was for?'

'To feed the dog if you must know.'

'So you keep dogs here on the farm? Do you think they might be responsible for the attack?'

'Could be, lass. We only have one dog. Let me call her in and you can see her for yourself. Bess! Bess, where are you? Get in here, Bess.'

There was a skittering of claws on concrete and a small Yorkshire Terrier made its way across the yard. It had a pink ribbon tied to keep its hair out of its eyes.

'This is Bess. Do you think she might bring down a cow? You're a clever copper you are.'

'There's a lot of meat here for a little dog like that, Mr Rounton. Are you sure you don't have any other animals on the property?'

'I've got 350 cows, 80 pigs, a dozen chickens and a fat goat, if that's what you're after. Do you want to take any of them in for questioning? Otherwise I've got work to do.'

'Well I won't keep you any longer then,' Terri said, and turned to leave. 'You know your sign's spelt wrong don't you?'

'What are you on about?'

'The sign for eggs as you come in. Did you write it?'

'What if I did? Don't need a licence to sell eggs do I?'

'Have you ever been tested for dyslexia, Mr Rounton?'

'There's nowt wrong with my digestion, now bugger off.'

Terri's radio chose this moment to crackle into life.

'PC Arswhistle, come in please. PC Arswhistle.'

'I'm here, Sarge, what is it?'

'Are you still up at Rounton Farm?'

'Yes, Sarge.'

'Ah good. We've had another call from that walker, Mr Daniels.'

'Not another smell is it, Sarge?'

'No. It sounds like he's got himself into a bit of bother. We didn't get the whole call; he got cut off part way through, but it sounds like he's in that same area up by Allerton Lane. Can you take a look?'

'I'll get over there now.'

'Thanks, Terri. I'll set off from the station and meet you there.'

Terri was glad to leave Rounton Farm behind. There was something not right about that place, she could feel it. It was getting late by the time she got to the field, but the bright full moon meant she had little trouble finding her way back up to the copse.

Inside the close thicket of trees, however, it was a different matter. Barely any light penetrated through the thick canopy and Terri had to use her police-issue torch to see anything at all. The stink hadn't changed though. That was still as strong as it had been earlier. It caught at the back of her throat and made her want to throw up again. The trees also blocked out most of the wind, making the copse still and quiet, and Terri became aware of the nocturnal sounds of birds, rabbits and a million insects. And then she heard it: a low growl coming from somewhere in the darkness. She moved her head, trying to work out the direction it was coming from. She swung the torch light around as she did so, but its weak beam only penetrated a few feet in front of her.

Then she heard another sound, a sharp hiss which seemed to be coming from somewhere up above her. For some reason she thought of the giant hissing cockroaches she had seen on a nature documentary; surely they couldn't survive in Yorkshire? She shone the torchlight up into the branches above her, on her guard in case a startled nest of hissing cockroaches came crashing down onto her head. She looked up and saw a man's face peering back down at her.

'Are you Mr Daniels? I'm from the police. I believe you made a call earlier this evening.'

'Oh thank God!' said the man. 'I thought I'd be up here all night.'

'How did you get up there anyway?'

'You could say I flew up here on the wings of terror.'

'Do you think you could fly back down again, sir?'

'I think so,' came the reply, followed by the sound of several branches breaking and a weighty thump as Mr Daniels crashed to the ground.

'Are you alright, sir?' asked Terri.

'I think so. I landed on something soft. I say, did you find out what that terrible smell was around here?' Terri guessed what he had landed in and thought it best to practice some diplomatic policing.

'We think it's a reaction from some organic fertilizer, sir; perfectly harmless, of course.'

'That's interesting,' Mr Daniels began, but he never got any further as they both became aware of a low, ominous growling coming from somewhere very close by.

'Oh my God,' whimpered Mr Daniels, 'it's come back.'

Terri whispered, 'I think we ought to get going, sir,' and helped him to his feet. They started to creep quietly back out of the woods. Then the growling started up again. It was closer, much closer. The animal panted in the darkness, readying itself for an attack.

'Quick,' said Terri, 'run!' and they charged blindly through the trees, snapping off branches and snagging their clothes on brambles until they could see the opening and the moonlit field beyond. Terri pushed Mr Daniels on in front of her. She could feel the creature close behind her, but they were going to make it. There were only a few more feet to go, when her foot caught on an old tin can lying on the ground. She tripped and fell heavily. A dark shape with red eyes and bared yellow teeth loomed over her. She swung the torch at it, but it ducked out of range. She swung again. The creature was too fast and pounced onto her chest. Terri clubbed it around the face with the torch, but it didn't have any effect. Its claws ripped at her uniform, sinking into the heavy stab vest. As she struggled, it tightened its grip. She tried to push it off, but it was too strong. It kept lunging for her face; its breath fetid. Suddenly, the weight was lifted, and she saw it twist round and snap at something behind it. Then the creature was raised high into the air and swung hard against a tree. There was a terrible crunch, and it dropped to the ground. Dead.

'Arswhistle! Arswhistle, are you alright?' She had never been more relieved to hear Rowbotham's voice.

'I'm fine, Sarge. Did Daniels get out?'

'He's with me. He stinks a bit but he's OK.'

'Best put him in my car then,' said Terri. 'I think this is going to stink it out anyway.' And she crashed through the trees and out into the moonlight dragging the carcass of a huge boar badger behind her.

'Did you do that, Arswhistle?'

'Weren't me, Sarge. But I think I know who it was. We need to pay another visit to Rounton's Farm.'

They got there to find Peter Rounton frantically throwing gristly meat and white pellets onto a bonfire.

'If I'd have known you were having a barbecue, I'd have brought some sausages,' said Rowbotham, picking up one of the bags of pellets and passing it to Terri. 'I don't think these firelighters of yours are much good though.'

'What I do on my own land is my business,' said Rounton. 'I ain't done nothing illegal.'

'What about these pellets?' said Terri. 'You seem keen to get rid of them.'

'Rat poison,' said Rounton. 'Same as all the other farmers use, only this batch didn't work proper.'

'You must have some bloody big rats,' said Rowbotham. 'There's enough here to poison half the county. Where did you get it?'

'From this bloke in the Farriers Arms.'

'I got it from a man down the pub?' said Terri. 'That's the oldest story going. I bet you'd never even seen him before.'

'No, I knew who it was. It was Jeannie Havergoe's lad, Alan. He told me he could order it for me wholesale off the computer. I just had to let him know what I needed.'

'Which was?'

'It's called metaldehyde. It's the same stuff everyone else uses.'

'And how did you order it, Mr Rounton?' said Terri.

'How did I order it? I wrote it on a bit of paper and he went off and sent for it.'

'You wrote it down?' said Terri. 'And you're sure you got it right?'

'What does it matter?' said Rounton. 'He got it didn't he?'

'And did you notice anything odd about this batch of rat poison?' asked Terri.

'Well the pellets were a bit different, but I thought that was because they were wholesale.'

'These aren't pellets, Mr Rounton, they're tablets,' said Terri.

'What are you on about?'

'This isn't rat poison,' said Terri. 'It's methylphenidate; they use it in psychiatric care.'

'How do you know that, Arswhistle?' asked Rowbotham.

'It has another use, Sarge. In dog fighting they give it to the animals to make them more aggressive. We had a spate of it in Leeds. Someone stole a big load of it from the hospital and sold it round the estates. It made the pit bulls psychotic. Do you want to tell us what you're doing with it, Mr Rounton?'

They were interrupted by the massive figure of Martin Rounton charging into the yard.

'Dad, Dad! There's police up at the wood!'

'Shut up, lad, and get indoors,' said Rounton, who did not look pleased to see his son.

'Stay where you are, son,' said Rowbotham. 'You ought to be nicer to this lad, Rounton. If he hadn't been around tonight, you might have been looking at a manslaughter charge. Or even murder.'

'You're making it up,' said Rounton. 'He's no bloody use to anyone.'

'That's where you're wrong,' said Terri. 'It was you wasn't it?' she said to Martin. 'In the woods, you pulled that big boar off me and killed it.'

'Don't say anything!' said Rounton.

'But, Dad,' said Martin. 'It's all right now. That was the last one.'

'The last what, Martin?' said Terri.

'The last badger, of course.'

'Bugger,' said Rounton. Rowbotham looked at Terri and raised his eyebrows. 'Go on then.'

'Peter Rounton,' said Terri. 'I'm arresting you under the Protection of Animals Act 1911. You do not have to say anything, but it may harm your defence if you do not mention when questioned something you later rely on in court.'

There was a lot of paperwork to go through that evening, not to mention signing a fifty-pound badger corpse into the evidence store.

'All done, Sarge,' said Terri, leaning back from her PC. 'I'll go and see Alan Havergoe tomorrow and see what he knows about those tablets.'

'Well done, Terri,' said Rowbotham. 'That was good police work today.'

'Thanks, Sarge. Do you think Martin will be all right? He won't get sent down will he?'

'Probably not,' said Rowbotham. 'Technically he is the one who laid the poison out, but he was clearly acting on his dad's instructions. There's provable guilt on one side and diminished responsibility on the other.'

Terri noticed his cheeks twitch, and a smile started to play around his lips. She knew what was coming and braced herself for the inevitable.

'You see, Arswhistle, even in a case about badgers, it's not all black and white.' And he was off. Tears streamed down his red face and his whole body shook with laughter.

'Yes, Sarge,' said Terri. 'I suppose he could get away by a whisker.' Well if you can't beat them, she thought, and left for home.

The Secrets of Calligraphy – Suz Winspear

Another evening, another art gallery. Another exhibition opening. And there I was as usual, with another glass of Hungarian merlot and a few crisps, trying my hardest to ignore the art. Nothing new there! After so many years attending events like this, I had learned that the things on the walls were the excuse to come, not the purpose. In my memory most of the exhibitions I'd been to had long since merged into one, anyway. That particular exhibition – I know it was a Friday night, but I can't remember the name of the artist. I think she came from Wolverhampton. Or was it Walsall? The works were small constructions in boxes, each one with an Artist's Comment on a label on the wall beside it, explanations that somehow seemed to make the work even less comprehensible than it was to start off with.

I'd seen it all before. So many times before!

Yes, I was jaded and bored, but I still kept on going to exhibition openings. Why? I suppose I needed to keep the semblance of life and vitality circulating in the provincial art scene. At times I felt like a small part in one of those machines used in hospitals to keep comatose patients alive. As I said, I was jaded and bored.

I drank my wine, went back for some more, and got on with the business of the evening. By which I mean, networking. I got into a conversation with a couple doing an Art in Education project, and gave them the e-mail address of someone I knew who was doing something similar. I chatted to someone else about a potential exhibition space in an empty shop and gave her the name of someone on the Council who was friendly to such schemes, and I met someone else who was looking for a studio, and promised to keep an eye open for anything appropriate … Networking … And eventually the guests went home, there was barely any wine left, the art had been steadfastly ignored in public for two hours, and there I was feeling a bit hazy, and wondering if I could finish off that last half-bottle of merlot before it all got cleared away. There was only one other person left in the gallery. He seemed as determined as me to stick it out until the end of the bottle, so we inevitably ended up by the drinks table together, and of course we began talking to fill in the awkwardness.

He was a tall thin young man. That's all I can say about him. Beyond that … I can't remember his face. At the time, I put this down to the wine. In retrospect, I'm not so sure … He started telling me about his work. He said he specialised in Extreme Body Art. In the haze of the merlot, most of the details escaped me, but I think meat hooks and rope bondage were involved, and I must have looked a bit queasy at that because he quickly poured me some more wine, and said, 'I do another type of art as well … would you like to see?'

Maybe it would have been sensible to have said no and gone home, but my instincts weren't to say no. They never are, not when art is involved. Maybe there was some part of me that still wasn't completely jaded; that hoped to see a work of art that would delight me once again. Maybe there was still that chance, even though I expected nothing but the usual disappointment.

Next thing I knew, he had a portfolio open in front of me. I wasn't sure where he'd been keeping it; I was sure he hadn't been holding one when we began the conversation. But there it was, and he started taking out artworks.

They were all on thick creamy-white paper that appeared to be handmade, and were done in a rusty red-black paint or ink, each one between twelve and eighteen inches square. But as for what they were … at first they just seemed to be dark smears, splashes and squiggles; only on a second glance I could see that the marks weren't random, that they had some sort of organising principle behind them, although I couldn't quite make out what it was. But there was something about them that nagged the mind. Something that almost seemed … how can I put it? … Watchful … Even in my befuddled state, there was something about these drawings that caught my attention. I was glad the artist just let me look at them without trying to tell me what they meant. I didn't want an explanation. I just wanted to look.

The artist then pulled one out from near the bottom of the pile and held it up in front of me.

'What do you think?' he said. 'Do you like this one?'

I looked at the smeared red-black marks that seemed to contain nothing and everything at the same time.

'Yes …' I said, feeling unable to think of anything more intelligent to say. 'I do.'

'Then it's yours,' he said, and gave it to me.

'Mine? … Are you sure?'

'Oh yes. This is the one for you … I mix the ink myself, you know. It has my own blood in it …'

I think the wine had really got to me by that stage. I don't remember what happened next or how the evening ended. There was a haze, and my next coherent memory I had was of standing on the pavement outside the gallery, with my coat, bag, and that strange gift of a drawing.

I got home somehow. The pavements accommodated themselves to my unsteady steps, as they so often do. I got home, put the drawing on the coffee table, and went straight to bed.

I woke up the next morning with the strange feeling that something had happened … I thought about it, and tried to remember whether I'd made an idiot of myself at the exhibition opening. After a bit of thought, I decided I hadn't done anything too bad. I remembered the artist, and his gift. But I couldn't recall his face, and only then did it occur to me that I hadn't even asked his name.

I got up, feeling a bit bleary and hung over, and went to have a look at my drawing. It was on the coffee table where I'd left it, but it didn't look quite as I'd remembered it. I wasn't entirely sure what was different about it. Maybe I was just looking at it the wrong way up.

I had a few cups of tea, listened to the news on the radio, then had a shower and made myself breakfast. Only after that did I go back to the drawing. It was definitely different. Different from how it had looked the night before; different from how it had seemed to be when I got up. I was sure the marks weren't quite as I remembered them. It seemed odd, but I was still a little too fragile to think about it very deeply, so I left the drawing on the coffee table and got on with my e-mails. After a while I went out to get some groceries, and did all those other dull necessary tasks that I could do without the capacity to think straight.

By lunchtime, my thoughts were sufficiently ordered for me to decide that I should try to find out something about that drawing, starting with who the artist was. There was no signature anywhere on the paper, but I took a photo in the hope that someone would recognise the style. I loaded the photo onto the computer and went around a few websites, but there was nothing to match. After an unsuccessful hour or so, I had another look at the original.

It didn't look like the photo any more.

In the time since I had taken the photograph, the drawing had changed its appearance. In the photo, there was a long smeary mark to one side, and smaller outbursts of ink coming out of it. But in the drawing in front of me, a gap like an eye had opened up in the centre of the smear, which was now squarish rather than long, and the other marks were organising themselves around it.

I took another photograph.

When I looked at the drawing again a few hours later, the ink was forming into a series of long dark worms, twisting around the central eye-like structure. Only that was now less like an eye than like some sort of galactic wormhole from a science fiction film, drawing everything into its empty white heart.

I took another photo, and for the next two days I took fresh photographs every half hour. Even throughout the night I came and took regular photos, catching a few minute's sleep in the intervals before the alarm clock buzzed again. When I finally looked at all the photos in sequence, I could see the way the image was moving around. It was never still, was always shifting into an unending variety of infinitely mutable shapes. But it was only when I borrowed a time-lapse camera from a friend that I really began to appreciate the activities of the bizarre drawing that I had been given. The movements weren't random. The inky markings were crawling around the paper with some sort of organised intelligence. When I was in the room, they flowed across the paper towards me. They were aware of my presence, and seemed interested in me, watching me like a pet animal in a cage. Their movements were too slow for me to see in real time, but when I watched the film I could see them. Alive … The drawing was alive.

At once I felt a peculiar sense of horror. This gift had turned out to be something sinister and unknowable, with its living ink smearing itself across the paper. I couldn't understand it, and I didn't like to be in the room with it.

After a couple of days, I couldn't stand it any more … The thought of this thing in my house, watching me all the time … thinking about me (was it able to think?) … it was freaking me out. I took the drawing and tore it in half. From the torn edges, the ink began to liquefy and drip reddish brown to stain the carpet. I remembered what the artist had said, about his blood being in the ink. The thought of it made my stomach churn queasily, and now I didn't want even the parts of the drawing anywhere near me. I took the two pieces and put them through the shredder. The markings began to writhe. The drawing knew what was happening, and in its panic it was flowing quickly enough for me to see, as I fed the paper into the machine. At the end of it I had a shredder-box of paper strips, all matted, sticky and stained with the thick blood-ink.

It looked like something from a crime-scene. I took the remains out to the bin and threw them away, and washed out and bleached the shredder-box and as much of the machine itself as I could get to, hoping to remove every sinister scrap, every drip of residue. My hands were covered with the foul ink, and I spent ages scrubbing them to get rid of it all.

I then went out for the day, feeling light and relieved that the drawing was gone.

But when I came home, there on the doormat on top of that day's junk mail, was a lightly-folded piece of thick handmade paper, bearing those strange red-black markings, and a note from one of my neighbours paperclipped to a corner. 'Found this outside your door. Is it yours?'

I'd thought I'd destroyed it, but it had come back. It seemed undamaged. I put it back on the coffee table, and turned the time-lapse camera back on to see if it was still alive. When I watched the footage a couple of hours later, I saw that it was, and I learnt something else about it. Whereas the ink had previously crawled towards me as though wanting to be close to me, now it shrank back. It tried to get as far away from me as possible, cringing like a whipped dog. I'd hurt it, and it was now afraid of me.

When I saw that, it upset me. I felt guilty for what I'd done. The drawing was creepy and unnatural, but not malign. It had liked me. From the way the artist had selected it as mine, I even wondered if it had chosen me. Certainly it had a sort of intelligence. It had known what I was doing to it. Maybe it was even capable of feeling pain. And I'd been cruel to it. I'd tortured it. I'd been horrible … But still it had come back to me. After all that, it had come back … A bottle and a half of red wine later, and I was on my knees in front of the coffee table, in tears, apologising to the drawing for what I'd done. I made a drunken promise to buy it a nice frame, and I said time and again that I would never ever do anything else to hurt it …

I woke up the next morning with a hangover and a sense of embarrassment at having made an idiot of myself in front of a drawing, but the time-lapse camera showed that it wasn't afraid of me anymore. It was suspicious, I think, but it didn't shrink back from me.

Over the next few days, we settled down into a routine, the drawing and I. I started talking to it, just casually, like some people talk to their pets, and I got the impression that it was paying attention. As to how much of what I said it could hear or understand, I was never certain, but it started to trust me again, judging by the way the ink crawled towards me once more, and took an interest in my activities. And I began searching on the internet for any clue as to what it really was. After a few days of trawling through the Google links for 'living drawings', I started to find other people who also had drawings like mine. Just one or two at first, but then more. Eventually I discovered a small community of about two dozen of us. Everyone had a similar story to mine; they had been approached by the strange artist whose face they couldn't remember, who had selected a drawing for them. A living drawing. We were spread throughout the world, with a few individuals scattered over every continent. There was someone in Germany, a couple of people in Japan, a few in America. One was in South Africa, another in Argentina; there was one in Sweden, and two in Australia. The artist had evidently travelled widely to distribute his drawings. And what did we have in common? Very little. Recipients were of all races, genders, star signs, blood-groups, sexual, religious and political orientations. Some were wealthy, some were poor. We all had different personality types. Only one thing connected us. We were all art-enthusiasts who had grown bored and disillusioned with art.

And who was this well-travelled artist? There were plenty of theories about that, but nothing that could be proved. Maybe he wasn't human at all. Surely no human could put in that many air miles? Who could afford to travel the world like that on an artist's salary? But nobody could say exactly what he was. An alien? An angelic spirit? A demon or a demi-god? Or something else entirely? Nobody knew.

And of course, everyone had their own theories about what these drawings were and how they were made. One person had taken his to a laboratory to have the ink analysed. He found out that it did contain a considerable proportion of blood that might have been human, but might not have been. But it had other constituents as well, chemical compounds that the scientists didn't recognise. A couple of recipients had, like me, tried to destroy their drawings. But the drawings couldn't be destroyed. Whatever was done to them, they had always returned. One was found undamaged in the ashes of a bonfire which had totally consumed a large heap of firewood, a rubber tyre and a chest of drawers, and its paper was as perfectly creamy-white as ever. Another had been ripped up and scattered from a speeding car. But still it had come back.

One person I spoke to had a theory that the drawings weren't really drawings at all, that they weren't just abstract images but some sort of calligraphy, and that by moving about, the ink was spelling out messages to communicate with us. But nobody knew the script, or ever learnt to interpret the meaning. We never found out what the messages were.

In time, I came to love my drawing. It gave the wonder and mystery back to my dried-out life. I fell in love with art again. When I went to exhibitions I looked at what was on the walls, just as I had done years ago, and sometimes felt delight at what I saw. A little bit of splendour and a little bit of strangeness had re-entered my disillusioned soul, and as long as I knew that there were things like those drawings in the world, I could never feel cynical, bored or jaded.

And then one day, I woke up and the drawing was gone. There was just a blank piece of paper; all the ink had disappeared. I e-mailed the other recipients. The same thing had happened to every one of them. All the drawings had gone. Every single one. Not a trace of ink was left anywhere. Some of the recipients speculated that the artist had died, but I think he'd just given up trying to communicate with us. We hadn't understood his messages or learned to read his script, so he'd taken back his gifts and left us. His drawings had returned the lost enchantment to our lives, but none of us had ever learnt the secrets of his calligraphy.

The Send Off – Tony Judge

It started, like so many improbable schemes, after a late night conversation in a pub. Three ageing men sat around a table, each clutching a pint in the latter stage of its life. Around them a small cemetery of dead glasses bore witness to the truth that no big idea is worth taking seriously unless preceded by some serious drinking.

Mac, Big Mac, with his military tache, slammed a heavy tattooed hand on the table, making all the unattached glasses jump. An ex-sergeant in the Paras, a leader of men, he nailed the plan for them.

'Right, it's settled. Anyone who wants to back out, say so now.'

He fixed Jimmy, the semiretired plumber, and then Bill, the unretired layabout, with his Falklands look.

'I'm in,' said Jimmy.

'Me too,' said Bill. 'It's what he would have wanted.'

'We'll have to move fast, then,' said Mac. 'He'll be in the ground come Wednesday.'

He wrote a list of kit for each of them: balaclavas, claw hammers, jemmy irons, torches, kindling and firelighters. The list went on.

'Blimey, what's this? Goose Green all over again,' quipped Bill.

Big Mac necked the last bit of his pint, flashing an angry sideways look at Bill as he drank.

'All right, mate. At ease. I told you, I'm in. We'll give him the send off he wanted and bollocks to Doreen and that poncy son of his.'

'See you both round the back of Co-op Funeral Care at 22.30 hours, sharp,' said Mac. He stood up and strode purposefully for the door; the dignity of his departure marred only by a slight collision with the doorframe on his way out.

'22 what?' said Bill, after Mac had gone.

'Half ten tomorrow night, you pillock,' said Jimmy.

The barman called last orders. Bill stood up and rooted in his pocket for change. After several seconds of this performance, Jimmy slapped a tenner down and pushed it towards him.

'What are we going to carry him in?' said Bill on his return from the bar.

'Mac says he has an old body bag stashed in his attic,' said Jimmy.

'Yeah, I bet he has. And people wonder why on earth Jenny left him.'

'It's a mystery.'

They smirked at one another.

The next night they met in the unlit car park. Under terse whispered orders from Mac, they executed the plan with all the proficiency of a slightly geriatric team of Navy Seals. They disabled the alarm and jemmied open a back window. Each of them squeezed through, grunting a little as their creaking limbs were forced into unaccustomed, youthful postures. Inside, they soon found Harry's casket, left open for more work on the morrow.

Their friend, dressed in a dark suit, lay with his arms crossed over his chest; his pale features set like a mask from a costume hire shop. Cosmetic work on the face was obviously still on the Co-op's to-do list.

'Christ, he looks like Count Fucking Dracula,' said Bill. 'Are you sure we're doing the right thing?'

'Are you ratting out on your mates?' growled Mac.

'No, no, course not. It's just that … well it's all a bit grim, a bit heavy.'

Jimmy, sensing that Mac was just about to launch into an 'until you've buried one of your mates after seeing him with half his face shot off, you don't know what grim is' speech, intervened.

'Look, we're committed now. Let's just get on with it.'

Bill steadied the coffin, while the others hefted Harry out and into the body bag. Mac patted the cold face before closing the last bit of the heavy gauge zip.

Getting Harry's dead weight through the window was a struggle: the bag snagged on the window catch, opening a large tear. A hand, still sporting a gold wedding ring, poked through the hole. Mac shoved it back in and resealed the bag with some duck tape. They loaded the body into the back of Jimmy's white Peugeot van, among all the plumbing gear.

'Couldn't you have cleaned it out first?' said Mac. 'Where's your respect, man?'

'Sorry, I didn't think.'

They drove slowly from the car park, trying not to attract attention.

Ten minutes later they drew up by the riverbank, near where Harry's narrow boat, his immaculately restored retirement project, was moored.

On a dank November night, the place was deserted.

A few minutes later the ceremony was prepared. Harry's body, bag removed, lay on the cabin roof, under him a pile of wooden pallets and kindling all soaked in diesel from Time To Play's capacious tank.

Jimmy read out a poem called Don't Bury Me; one of Harry's last, written when The Grim Reaper's SatNav had Harry's postcode stored under favourite locations. Their friend's desire for a particular style of funeral was clearly expressed.

'I'll not be buried in the ground.
A narrow wooden box would be
a resting place far too earthbound.
Thin worms shall not grow fat on me.

I don't want horses in black plumes

or a gleaming silver bier.
I don't want relatives in rooms
struggling so hard to shed a tear.

I will depart as a Viking
upon a dragon-prowed longship.
Such an end is to my liking;
fine transport for the final trip.

Slaughter your cat (but spare my dog).
Lay it out, prone along the deck.
My gaunt ship drifting through the fog,
shrinking to a fiery speck.'

'Shit. We've forgotten the cat,' said Bill, after a respectful pause.

Mac reached into a bulging pocket in his camouflage jacket and pulled out a stiff bundle. He tossed it onto the pyre next to Harry.

'You didn't?' said Bill, staring in horror at Mac.

'It's what he wanted,' said Mac.

'Such a lovely boat,' said Bill. 'His pride a joy … seems a shame to burn it. Can't we just put him in the rubber dinghy?'

'Numpty,' said Mac. 'It'll sink in seconds and his body'll wash up on the beach at Weston in a couple of weeks.'

'You're right,' said Bill. 'It's what he would have wanted, to go off down the river on his lovely boat in a final blaze of glory.'

Mac put the engine in gear and secured the wheel with a car steering lock. The narrow boat strained against the stern rope that was still fastened to the jetty.

'Who's going to light it?' said Jimmy.

Mac reached into another pocket, pulled out three sticks with rags tied around the ends and lit each one.

'After three,' he said. 'One, two, three,' and they threw the firebrands towards Harry.

In seconds a huge conflagration caught hold along the entire length of the boat, blistering at the paintwork applied with such care over the years.

'Mac, exactly how much diesel did you use?' said Jimmy.

'Maybe a bit too much. Abandon ship!'

A scramble for the gangplank ensued. Mac cut the rope and the Time To Play lurched out into the swirling brown water; a mobile pyrotechnic display.

'Just what Harry wanted,' he muttered and turned to look at the others.

'Where's Bill?' he said.

'I thought he came off before you,' replied Jimmy.

In the distance, a shadowy pair of arms gesticulated frantically from the already blazing wheelhouse.

'Jump, you pillock, jump!' shouted Mac in a parade ground bellow.

'Oh shit,' said Jimmy. 'He can't swim.'

The Time To Play shrank to a fiery speck, rounded a bend in the river and passed away out of sight.

'Oh God. That's terrible,' said Mac.

'Yeah, terrible. Bastard still owes me a tenner,' said Jimmy.

The Werewolf Curse – Kevin Brooke

It's hard to imagine my first hunt was only a month ago: the chase through the trees in the dark, the piles of fallen leaves grabbing at my ankles and slowing me down, while the pounding of the wolves' feet grew ever closer.

I don't know how we escaped. Zak says it was down to him – HIS cunning, HIS awareness of the situation that led us to the river where we swam to safety in the freezing water. Some of the others weren't so lucky, and I can still hear their screams as the wolf pack descended upon them and ripped them apart.

I remember heaving myself out of the water; the feeling of relief at the orange glow of the rising sun confirming I would survive for at least another month.

Twenty-eight days later and that same sun was about to set behind the tall pine trees at the edge of the forest. The werewolf curse was set to return, and all those over the age of twenty would feel the pain of the transformation. The rest of us would have to make a decision: to hide or to hunt.

Zak passed me the dark mixture he'd been preparing. It was a kind of oil dosed in Monkshood, the classic wolf deterrent.

'Cover every exposed piece of flesh, Calum,' he said. 'Just enough to prevent the wolves from getting too close. Too much and you'll scare them off completely.'

Until I met Zak I'd always been one of those who'd hidden. My survival philosophy had always been that if I didn't provoke them they'd leave me alone in return, at least for the next five years until it was my turn for the monthly transformation from man to wolf.

Just two moons ago the wolves altered my outlook forever. I was hidden in a padlocked hut with four other hiders and three of the younglings, the prepubescent who are supposedly protected from harm.

As the wolves circled the hut, one of the hiders lifted a sobbing child to the window, confirming we were protecting the younglings from the evils of the night. Instead of moving on to other prey, however, the wolves smashed the padlock and barged through the opened door.

Saliva dripping through the gaps in their teeth, the wolves paused for a moment. Then, their shadows lengthening across the floor, they edged towards us as we huddled together in the corner, slowly enough for us to feel their hunger and desire. The hider who'd lifted the youngling to the window charged towards them – he had no choice. I remember the silver of his sword flashing in the moonlight as he struck at the hind legs of the first wolf. The injured beast slumped onto the wooden floor, howling in pain as his skin smoked from the effects of the silver, the smell of burnt flesh making me retch.

The rest of the pack circled the hider and then, as one, aimed their menacing eyes at the terrified group in the corner. With scrabbling claws and bared teeth the wolves dived amongst us, the shrieks of panic echoing around the hut as they attacked hiders and younglings alike.

I tensed, waiting for the pain of razor sharp canines ripping the flesh from my bones, but the dreaded moment never came. Instead, the wolves retreated under a flurry of arrows and spears. It was Zak and his fellow hunters.

Of the eight of us who'd huddled in the corner of the hut, I was the only one to survive. The younglings were killed outright, their forbidden flesh proving too tasty, too succulent for the wolves to resist. Two of the older hiders were still alive, but they'd been bitten and the transformation had begun. Zak killed them both before they had the chance to beg him to do so; the pain of the change from boy to wolf at too young an age would have killed them anyway. Even so, I was appalled by his heartlessness.

My time as a hider was now firmly behind me. Zak saving my life was reason enough for me to join him, but the forbidden killing of the younglings made me realise I had no choice. My only concern about that night was how Zak and his fellow hunters were able to get there so quickly. It was almost as though they were watching and waiting for the moment when the wolves were attacking us and at their most vulnerable. I later convinced myself their arrival at the critical moment was a case of sheer good fortune.

'It's time, Calum,' said Zak. He had a silver amulet covering his right forearm and a bow slung from his shoulder, the silver tipped arrows in a quiver by his side. My second hunt was about to begin.

'Should I take a weapon? A spear maybe?' I asked.

'There's no need. This is not part of your role tonight.'

I nodded, even though I wasn't convinced by his answer. What was my role if it wasn't the killing of werewolves?

He noticed my concern. 'If you must take something, then take some wolfsbane, but make sure you keep it well hidden.'

I grabbed some yellow, helmet-like flowers from the plant he'd pointed at and stuffed them deep into my pocket. Moments later we left the cover of his shelter, out into the night air. October had been particularly cold and tonight was no exception.

Heads bowed, we started to run. I flinched at an ear-piercing howl in the distance, and looked towards Zak for reassurance. He didn't look back, but stared straight ahead as though readying himself for the battles to come. Together, we headed into the woods, the sweet, soothing smell of evening pine helping my troubled mind for a moment.

'There's our trail,' he said, the indentation on the fifth toe of the front paw prints clearly distinguishing the wolf spoor from that of a dog. 'Wait here.'

I knew we would eventually come into contact with the wolves who only hours before would have been people, just like us. I'd see them in the street, in church on Sundays, or at school where some were our teachers. One night a month it all changed, and so it would continue until the balance between food and population was restored. Only then would the curse be lifted; until then, the killing would continue. No one knew when that would be. No one questioned it any more.

I crouched lower into the foliage as another piercing howl echoed around the forest. It carried past my cowering body. I lifted my head to locate its origin.

Only ten or fifteen feet away, a huge black wolf stood proudly on a grey rock. When he saw me he lifted his head and pointed his nose towards the clouds in the night sky.

'Run,' I shouted at myself, in an effort to break the suffocating tension. I heard my frantic panting as I ran past the first tree, its lower branches shredding the skin of my upper arm. I glanced down at the blood seeping from the wound, my terror increasing at the memory of how the wolf pack had reacted to the smell of human blood. I didn't see the obstruction, and fell to the ground, dizzied and disorientated.

I searched frantically in my pockets for the wolfsbane. A blur of black fur flew above me and then slumped in a heap nearby, silver arrows protruding from its belly.

'Get up.' Zak grabbed at my collar, his fingers pinching my skin. 'There is more to do tonight.'

I looked at the dead wolf and then at Zak. He'd been nowhere to be seen and then suddenly on hand to kill the black wolf. I pieced things together. It was the same reason he and the rest of his hunters reached the hut so quickly that horrible night when the younglings were slaughtered. On both occasions Zak had used me as bait. I tried not to believe it, but there was no way it could be otherwise, the timings were just too precise.

In that moment I knew that in order to survive I would have to be as cold-hearted as the rest of them. With an electric charge of anger surging through me, I went to confront Zak, to challenge his methods. But as I approached he doubled up in pain. It didn't take much to work out what was wrong: the teeth marks of a wolf were clearly visible on his shoulder. He took his knife out from his belt and handed it to me.

'Please, make it quick.'

I stabbed him through the heart.

Watchers – Tana Durham

The watchers saw the builders wave to the woman before climbing into their pick-up and driving off. They saw Jane Delaney return the greeting as she slammed her car door.

Jane felt her skin prickle. She could see no one. After living in the house for three months, she felt no nearer to getting to know her neighbours despite her best efforts. Maggie from across the road was the only one who had exchanged more than a couple of words with her. She had invited Jane for coffee a few days after they'd moved in.

'How are you settling in?' Maggie had asked.

'Not well really. I'm missing my family and friends. I get this creepy feeling … I know this sounds silly but … has anyone around here … ever mentioned ghosts?'

Maggie had looked at her as if she were mad. 'In a new house, on an estate that's still being built? Of course not. What makes you say that?'

'Oh, little things. Nothing I can pin down. And people seem … wary.'

'It's your imagination. Everybody's friendly here,' Maggie had replied stiffly.

'I'm sure you're right. I'm being over sensitive.' Jane had forced a laugh and changed the subject.

Since then Jane and Rob shared the occasional drink and gardening tips with Maggie and her husband, Jim, when Rob was home on his two weeks leave from the rig.

Today Jane felt familiar apprehension as she put her key in the lock. She hovered on the threshold before stepping inside. *Let everything be normal.*

'Em,' she yelled up the stairs, 'come and help with dinner.'

No answer. Yet there was something.

Cautiously she opened the kitchen door. Chaos. Every drawer and cupboard was open. Bread, crumbs, jam everywhere. *For goodness sake, why can't kids tidy up after themselves?*

Brushing the mess away, she inspected the worktop. *Oh no! Deep scratches across my new work surface.* She heard the front door open. Girls voices, then silence.

Right, she thought wiping her hands, *I'm not accepting any excuses this time.* Emma and her friend were searching through the post on the hall table.

'Em, the mess you've left in here is a disgrace. The worktop is ruined. You'll have to contribute to a new one.'

Emma turned furiously to her mother. 'I haven't made a mess. I've been at Shona's. Anyway, where's the CD I left here? Shona wants it back.'

'I haven't seen it.'

'You must have. It was here. I brought it down this morning,' she said, with studied patience.

'I have not moved it, Emma. Now say goodbye to Shona. Dad is driving home tonight from Aberdeen and I need your help.'

* * *

'That smells delicious,' Rob said. 'What is it?'

'Chicken casserole.'

He nuzzled into Jane's neck. 'Mmm, casserole smells good too.'

She laughed and pushed him away. 'Here open this. Pour us a glass while I dish out.'

'Is Em alright? Where is she anyway?'

'Upstairs, hating me. She's OK, I think. I'll tell you later.'

After they had finished eating, Em started clearing the table. 'That was lovely Mum. I'll sort this. You two can go and watch TV if you like.' She gave Jane a hug and added, 'Sorry about before.'

'It's OK. I didn't move your CD though.'

'I know. I found it in my bedside cupboard. I could have sworn …'

'I think I'll go up,' Rob said. 'It was a bad drive back. I'm shattered. Come up soon?' he said, looking at his wife.

'I'll help Em first.'

'Honestly, Mum. It's OK. I'll lock up.'

'Be sure you do. School tomorrow, so get to bed before nine o'clock.' Jane laughed as Em pushed her towards the stairs.

Jane woke suddenly. A noise. A creaking hinge. She looked at the time. *Three o'clock. Surely Emma can't still be up?*

She stood at the top of the stairs, holding her breath. Silence. She looked in to Emma's room and saw she was fast asleep.

'Rob, wake up. There's someone downstairs.'

He groaned. 'There can't be. Go back to sleep.'

'There is. Maybe Em forgot to lock up.'

Rob appeared at her side, yawning.

Jane's heart thumped as, staying close to the wall, they crept down the stairs. Rob tried the front door. Locked. He selected a club from his golf bag and, keeping Jane behind him, edged towards the kitchen. They listened for a few seconds. Nothing. Jim flung the door back and jumped into the room with a yell, brandishing the golf club like a sabre. Jane smothered her urge to laugh. The kitchen was empty and immaculate. *Well done, Em.* She checked the back door. It was locked too. A search of the other rooms revealed nothing.

'You've dreamt it.'

'I was sure. Oh I don't know. There have been so many strange things happening since we moved here. Maybe I am paranoid.'

They drank tea while Jane told him about everything else.

'It's just little things. Stuff out of place. Every day for a couple of weeks. Then nothing for a while. Things go missing. Sometimes they reappear, but in odd places.'

'What sort of things?'

'Nothing valuable. Dangly earrings you got me in Spain. Money – mostly small change I think. Some underwear, but then I think it could have blown off the line. I can reason it all out. Except for the toilet.'

'What about it?'

'I got back from work one day and found it in a terrible state.'

Rob laughed. 'One of you forgot to flush?'

'No, Rob, you should have seen it.'

'Do you think …? Not Em?'

'I hope not. Perhaps her friends? She swears not.' Jane took a deep breath. *Now or never.* 'This is really going to sound crazy, but I've been reading about poltergeists. Perhaps …? I mean aren't they supposed to attach themselves to teenage girls? A sort of manifestation of negative energy, especially when there has been emotional upheaval. The move here, so far from everyone we know. I feel the strain myself …' Jane tailed off as she watched Rob's expression grow more incredulous.

He held Jane's hand between his and said, 'I can't see that in Em. One thing is certain, we won't solve anything tonight. Let's try and get some sleep.'

The following week was uneventful. The family settled into happy normality. Rob gardened and cooked meals for the family. After dinner they played board games, or watched DVDs or went out for a walk. Emma was in a particularly sunny mood.

'She's so happy to have you back. We both are. I wish …'

'Jane, two weeks on, two weeks off is weird I know, but I'd never get the chance to earn the same in a nine-to-five. Let's see how it goes. If it gets too bad …'

The day Rob drove to Aberdeen to catch his flight to the rig was the first cool day after a long warm spell. Thick fog rolled in from the sea. It hung undisturbed in the unusually still air and made flight impossible. Local weather services forecast the situation would remain unchanged for several more days. Rob was told to head back home and stay there until conditions improved.

He arrived late in the afternoon. He wasn't surprised to find the house quiet. Jane sometimes didn't get back from work until six o'clock and Emma often had after school clubs. He went in to the kitchen. *Blimey, they left in a bit of a hurry this morning didn't they?* He put the kettle on and started to wash up. *How did they manage to use every mug we own? Did Emma bring some friends back at lunchtime?*

Rob made himself a coffee and wandered into the lounge to drink it. *What's happened here? It looks as if a bomb has hit it.* Another thought shocked him into action. *Jane's poltergeist. She will be back soon. If she sees this lot she'll hit the roof.*

He tidied away the magazines and replaced the furniture where he thought it belonged. He didn't want Emma to get into any more trouble. He had the table set and a meal waiting when his wife and daughter arrived. They were so delighted he was home that if they noticed anything out of place, no one mention it.

The next morning Rob woke early. He sat up and tried to focus his eyes. Gradually, it dawned on him he was looking at a perfectly spherical black shape on the opposite wall. *What the…?*

'Jane, wake up!' he said, shaking her.

'What's the matter?' she muttered, squinting at the clock. 'Too early … go back to sleep.'

'No. Sit up and look. What's that?' He pointed at the wall.

Jane struggled onto one elbow and peered. 'I don't know. I've not seen it before. What does it look like to you?'

'This sounds crazy, but I think it's mud. It looks like someone threw a filthy football at the wall.'

'What? How can that be? It doesn't make sense.' Jane took a sharp breath as another thought struck her. 'Not visitors in the night?'

'We'd have heard I think. No, we just didn't notice when we came to bed.'

'But how did it get there?'

Remembering the chaos of the day before, Rob said, 'I think we must ask Emma.'

Despite gentle, but persistent questioning, Emma maintained it was nothing to do with her or her friends. The puzzling events stopped soon after the football incident. Jane and Rob chose to believe Emma and quietly let the subject drop. It seemed that the mystery would never be solved.

Eventually, the family moved away. Years later they bumped into Maggie and Jim. Over a drink they chatted over old times.

'We moved too,' said Jim

'We didn't like being overlooked,' added Maggie.

Jane laughed. 'I know. It's hard not to see everything that goes on in a cul-de-sac.'

After a pause Maggie said, 'We used to watch those builders go into your house.'

'We never had builders in.'

'Yes. Every lunchtime. Sometimes more often. They had a key. They only stopped when they moved to another site.'

Jane and Rob stared at each other in shocked silence. Long buried fears bubbled to the surface. *Poor Emma.*

'And you never thought to tell us?' Jane said. 'Why?'

Maggie just shrugged.

While We Were Out – Andrew Owens

'She's already eaten,' I said, 'but if she complains that she's hungry, she can have a snack before bed. Toast or cereal, but no chocolate. She can watch TV until eight o'clock, then get her to read you a story. She needs to be in bed by eight thirty at the latest. There's pop in the fridge and I've left a selection of crisps out for you on the counter. You have our number and if you have any problems, don't hesitate to call.'

'We'll be back before eleven,' my husband, Roger, added.

'Eight thirty to bed and no chocolate, got it,' Serafina said, as we put our coats on in the hallway.

'Okay, I think we're ready. Ready?' Roger nodded. From the doorway I called out to our nine-year-old daughter, who we had left sitting in front of the TV,

'We're going now, Wendy. Be a good girl for Serafina.'

Wendy was too engrossed in her programme to reply.

'Everything will be fine, Mrs Redfern. Have a good night,' Serafina said, as we stepped out of the door.

Nervously, I climbed into the passenger side of the car. I couldn't seem to get comfortable in my seat. Gazing into the wing mirror, I watched Serafina waving goodbye. As we pulled off the drive, she closed the door, which turned my attention to the way ahead.

'Do you think she'll be okay?'

'Yes,' Roger answered.

'How can you be so sure?'

'Look, just because it didn't work out with the last babysitter, it doesn't mean that it won't with this one.'

I wasn't convinced, despite his reassuring glance. I felt anxious and my fretful manner continued even after we were seated at the restaurant.

'Will you please stop playing with your napkin?' Roger whispered. 'We're here to relax and enjoy ourselves, not to fret about our daughter and the babysitter. It's been three months since we last went out and you agreed to this, so will you at least pretend to be having a good time?'

I put the table napkin on my lap and picked up the menu. The restaurant had clearly tried to make the menu attractive and inviting, but I couldn't focus on it. Unlike the napkin, I couldn't place my worries elsewhere. I needed reassurance.

'I need to call home,' I said, laying the menu down. Roger watched me leave the table with a reluctant nod.

Standing in the entrance hall, I took my mobile phone out from my handbag and selected 'home' from the contacts list. I became more anxious with each ring, but my nervousness was swiftly eased once my call had been answered.

'Hello? Redfern residence, Serafina speaking.'

Breathing a sigh of relief, I replied, 'Hi, Serafina. I was just ringing to see if everything is alright.'

'Everything's fine, Mrs Redfern. I made Wendy some toast and now we're going to watch some TV together. Are you and Mr Redfern enjoying your night out?'

'Yes, great thanks. The restaurant's nice and we're just about to order. I'd better go. You and, Wendy enjoy your show and I'll ring later. Thanks, Serafina.'

Back at our table, I found a waiter at Roger's side. Sitting down, I ordered and Roger watched me shuffle my chair closer to the table.

'And?' he asked, taking a sip of water.

'Everything's fine. Wendy's watching TV and will be going to bed soon.'

'See? I told you it would be all right.'

'Yes, I can relax now, but I'll ring again before we leave.'

To my joy, I finally felt I could put my worries aside and embrace the peace and pleasurable surroundings. Roger and I were able to enjoy enticing food and stimulating conversation over the next two hours, which seemed to pass so freely. I felt contented, elated even, to the extent that I became flirtatious. It had been a wonderful night out and now I was eager to return home, but not for reasons of getting back to our daughter or for sleep.

Roger, ever the gentleman, helped me with my coat as we prepared to leave. Taking my phone out from my handbag, I said, 'I'll just ring, Serafina to tell her that we're on our way.'

With my ear pressed to my mobile, I waited for her to answer my call. After seven rings the messaging service cut in and my stomach began to turn.

'She's not answering.'

'She's probably gone to the bathroom or she's in the kitchen making something to eat. Try again in the car.'

When Serafina didn't answer the phone on the journey home, my heart started racing and I had to hold onto the seat to stop myself shaking.

'Something's wrong,' I said. This time Roger didn't look so calm.

'I'm sure everything will be fine. Serafina will be sat on the sofa with her feet up, listening to her iPod. You know how young people are,' Roger said, concentrating on the road and trying to hide the waver in his voice.

We pulled into our drive. The lights were on, the curtains were drawn and the neighbourhood was peaceful, little preparation for what faced us inside.

I could hear the TV from the hallway, and the unmistakeable sound of the cartoon network.

Roger and I crept towards the living room. There was our daughter, sat in the middle of the room amongst a half dozen empty chocolate wrappers, with the babysitter lying next to her in a pool of blood

'Oh my God!' I yelled, but in spite of my shriek, Wendy didn't turn around. Instead, she remained fixed on the TV and was as silent as the body beside her.

Roger went over to her and asked, 'Wendy, what happened?' She didn't answer.

At first I couldn't speak, but a few seconds later it all came out.

'Just look at the mess she's made. She's ruined the carpet. I'll never get any of this out. She's even got it on the sofa!'

'There's no need to worry about the sofa, it's leather, it will wipe clean. As for the carpet, well that's a write-off and we won't be able to claim this on the insurance. What concerns me is what I'm going to do with the body? I'm running out of garden space.'

'Why, Wendy, why?'

'I don't watch those kinds of programmes,' Wendy replied. 'I wanted to watch Super Snork, she wanted to watch West End Street. All that boring yakety yak. She wouldn't change it back, so I went to the kitchen, got a knife and stabbed her. When she died, I figured that I was going to get into trouble anyway, so I ate the chocolate.'

'You got that right! You're grounded, you hear? Grounded!' I yelled. 'You can forget about seeing your friends or going to Cathy's birthday party next week, and you won't be using the computer. All I asked was for you to be good for one night, one night, so that your dad and I could have an evening out. Go to your room. Mind the blood; I've got enough to clean as it is already. I've got to sit down.'

Six months later, the phone rang. Picking it up I said, 'Hello?'

'Yeah hi, my name is Bryga. I'm calling in response to the ad in the paper …'

Author Biographies

Mike Alma: I have been interested in writing, both prose and poetry, all my adult life – fifty years of writing for the very joy of expressing myself … no more. For the last two years I have been encouraged to share my efforts with like-thinking folk and to hear and read the results of their endeavours. I thoroughly enjoy the company of some lovely people while involved, myself, in something pleasurable and worthwhile – writing.

Kevin Brooke writes fiction for both children and adults. He has a book aimed at 6-10 year olds, called *The Roman Citizens from Class 6B*, which is published on Amazon as an e-book and Lulu as a paperback. A second children's book, called *Jimmy Cricket*, this time aimed at early teens, is due to be completed in early 2014. He is a member of Worcester Writers' Circle and regularly performs his adult fiction at '42', a spoken word event based in Worcester, as well as being involved in short story events at the last three Worcestershire Literary Festivals.

Tim Butler is a writer of short, tall and long tales who lives and works in Worcester. He uses the profits from his thriving literary career to fund his hobby of commercial software development, and dreams of the day when he can give up writing altogether and concentrate fully on office life. He is the award winning author of The Brunts School Best Camp Diary, taking the title in Weymouth 1986 and The Isle of Mull in 1987. However, as so often happens with child prodigies, Tim fell subsequently into obscurity for many years and produced work sporadically while working on his first novel, *Scenes of Mild Peril.*

Alan Durham is an old bloke who writes a bit. He enjoys writing short stories and the occasional rhyming thing. Currently he is working towards the completion of his first novel, *The Hen Race*, which, if he gets his act together, he hopes to publish mid 2014. As he believes in the power of words, he is an active committee member of Worcestershire Lit Fest and Fringe, a member of Worcester Writers' Circle and the U3A Creative Writing Group. He enjoys watching the world walk by while drinking red wine at pavement cafés and eating things he knows he shouldn't.

Tana Durham: Somehow adventure winds itself around Tana's life. She rarely discusses her days as the private detective who exposed a Belgian rival as a conman and murderer. Or how on her 'Round the World on a Pogo Stick Challenge' she overthrew the mutinous crew of a Turkish gulet using only her pogo, so saving the life of the handsome captain. In the Andes, she bartered a bacon sandwich for a necklace of golden rocks strung on sinews of huja vine. The rocks were – rocks. Fortunately, the vine later proved to be a cure for pogo posterior.
Tana enjoys writing fiction.

Rod Griffiths: I spent my working life in Public Health, where the main task was to try to guess what might happen next, write a plan to deal with it, and then persuade people to spend money on the plan. Fiction writing on the other hand, is about trying to guess what might happen next, write a story or a book about it, and persuade people to spend money on the book. Same old same old really. So far I have two novels out, and I'm working on two more.

Tony Judge writes novels, short stories, satire and poetry. His first novel, *Sirocco Express*, describes the experiences of a young Nigerian student at the hands of people smugglers while travelling from Lagos to London. In his second novel, *The Whole Rotten Edifice*, a historical fiction set during the desperate defence of Moscow in 1941/2, a father and daughter serve in the Red Army. Tony's satires have been broadcast by Radio Wildfire. He is the author of several non-fiction books, published by BWCS and ARCchart, and is a member of the UK Society of Authors.

Andy Kirk is a magician, entertainer and writer. He writes short stories, poetry, flash fiction, and has recently turned his hand to writing short, mainly humorous, plays. He's only been writing for four years, but in that time he's been published in magazines, anthologies and on-line forums. He's also managed runner-up position in two flash fiction competitions and made top ten in the Worcestershire Literary Festival's competition. His play *The Spirit Catcher* has been aired on Radio Wildfire. Andy hopes he brings a bit of magic into everything he writes.

Damon Lord writes speculative fiction and poetry and lives and works in Worcester. Unlike the stereotypical writer, he does not like cats. Damon has been writing fiction since the age of six, and was exiled from his homeland of Wales for the inexcusable crime of not being interested in rugby. His website is www.damonlord.net

Alison May was born and raised in North Yorkshire, but now lives in Worcester with one husband, no kids and no pets. There were goldfish once. That ended badly. Alison has studied History and Creative Writing, and has worked as a waitress, a shop assistant, a learning adviser, an advice centre manager, and a freelance trainer, before settling on 'making up stories' as an entirely acceptable grown-up career plan. Alison is a member of the Romantic Novelists' Association. She writes short stories and contemporary romantic comedies. Her debut novel, *Much Ado About Sweet Nothing*, is out now.

Andrew Owens regularly performs at spoken word events throughout the West Midlands. He has had several short stories published in anthologies, magazines and online, and recently completed his first collection of short stories. Andrew was born and raised in Canada. He lives in Worcester, is married and has three children.

Dunstan Power is a freelance writer from Worcester. He writes flash fiction, short stories and is currently nearing the end of his first novel. His preferred genres are SF and contemporary fiction.

Polly Robinson is a member of Worcester Writers' Circle and part of the Worcestershire Literary Festival team. She enjoys performing her poetry at spoken word events such as Worcester SpeakEasy, 42 Worcester and Mouth & Music. Her writing has been published in many anthologies, most recently *The dVerse Anthology: Voices of Contemporary World Poetry* published this year. Polly released her first collection of poetry, *Girl's Got Rhythm*, in 2012. There's more to see at: http://journalread.wordpress.com Polly's blog, and her new poetry collection, simply entitled *Chatterton*, will be out as a pamphlet via Black Pear Press in 2014.

Suz Winspear lives in a disused church, works in a Victorian museum, and writes Gothic monologues and poetry, which she performs in a strikingly visual style. Her work has previously appeared in *Dark Tales* and *Ripples: Friends in Verse*, and her first collection of poetry, *I do not Need a New Obsession*, was published in 2013. She spends a lot of time making unusual costumes and listening to little-known Japanese bands.